[signature]

Maria Kellerman

Joan Lowery Nixon

Nicole Marie Brush

Annie A. Anderson

Carole Nelson Douglas

🐾

Midnight Louie, Esq.

[signature]

Alyson Hornsby

Max Allan Collins

Nate Collins

Sharyn McCrumb

Spencer McCrumb

Layla McCrumb

Ed Gorman

Jon Gorr

Eve Turow

Brian D'Amato

Barbara D'Amato

Lucy Kaminsky

Stuart M. Kaminsky

Patricia Wallace

Christina Wallace

Elizabeth Engstrom

Niède Sarragle

Billie Sue Mosiman

Suzanne Mosiman Garcia

GREAT WRITERS & KIDS WRITE
MYSTERY STORIES

EDITED BY MARTIN H. GREENBERG
JILL M. MORGAN AND ROBERT WEINBERG
WITH ILLUSTRATIONS BY
GAHAN WILSON

RANDOM HOUSE 🏠 NEW YORK

Special thanks to:

Random House senior editor: Alice Alfonsi
Random House assistant art director: Robert W. Kosturko
Random House senior designer: Jan Lebeyka

Additional thanks to Don Maass and the Don Maass Literary Agency,
and to Harold Clarke, Kate Klimo, and Cathy Goldsmith of Random House.

Photo credits: Jerry Kohn, p.14; Mel Reingold, p.32; Buddy Meyers, p.46; Lee B. Phan, p.62; Barbara Collins, p.78; Photography by Glenn, p.90; Carol Gorman, p.106; Annette Turow, p.118; Paul D'Amato, p.130; Vern Sawyer, p.144; Evan Engstrom, p.182; Lyle D. Mosiman, p.200.

Library of Congress Cataloging-in-Publication Data:
Great writers & kids write mystery stories / edited by Martin H. Greenberg, Jill M. Morgan, and Robert Weinberg ; with illustrations by Gahan Wilson.
   p. cm.
Contents: What makes a good mystery story / [introd.] by Jill M. Morgan and Robert Weinberg—Dog collar / Carole Nelson Douglas and Annie A. Anderson—The chocolate-chip alarm / Max Allan and Nathan Collins—Matinee / Jonathan and Ilana Kellerman—The secret enchanted dress / Scott and Eve Turow—Typewriter man / Sharyn, Spencer, and Laura McCrumb—Too violent / Barbara and Brian D'Amato—Relevé / Patricia and Christina Wallace—Moxie and the African Queen / Elizabeth Engstrom and Nicole Engstrom Fourmyle—The real-life adventures of Manny Fitz / Billie Sue Mosiman and Suzanne Mosiman Garcia—Owlie Madison / Ed and Joe Gorman—Be your own best friend / Wendy and Alyson Hornsby—Mother knows best / Stuart and Lucy Kaminsky—The disappearance of Gavin McCann / Joan Lowery Nixon and Nicole Marie Brush.
Summary: A collection of thirteen original tales by authors of adult fiction in collaboration with their children or grandchildren.
ISBN: 0-679-87939-0 (trade) — ISBN: 0-679-97939-5 (lib. bdg.)
1. Detective and mystery stories, American. 2. Children's stories, American. 3. Children's writings, American. [1. Mystery and detective stories. 2. Short stories.] I. Greenberg, Martin Harry. II. Morgan, Jill M. III. Weinberg, Robert E. IV. Wilson, Gahan, ill.
PZ5.G6976   1996
813'.087208—dc20
[Fic]
96-4602
Printed in the United States of America   10 9 8 7 6 5 4 3 2 1

CONTENTS

WHAT MAKES A GOOD MYSTERY STORY?

By Jill M. Morgan
and Robert Weinberg

When you think of a mystery, what comes to mind? A dark secret? An unsolved crime? A curious detective hunting for clues?

At the heart of every good mystery story is some kind of *secret, riddle,* or *puzzle.* Trying to discover the truth of the secret, answer the riddle, or solve the puzzle is what makes a mystery fun to read. But how do you, the reader, go about doing this?

The first thing to do is to look for *clues.*

Clues are a very important part of a mystery story. They are like pieces to the story's overall puzzle. The author plants the clues in such a way that if you pay attention you can put them together and solve the mystery. Clues are usually revealed one by one, all through the tale.

Fans of mystery stories enjoy the process of finding the clues. They want to guess the identity of the guilty party, or discover the answer to the story's riddle, *before* they get to the last page.

A good mystery story often leads the reader down some wrong paths. These false clues are called *red herrings.* They make the task of solving the puzzle even more difficult. But when the author presents these wrong clues, he or she must do it fairly. The author should never trick the reader.

Good mystery stories are like a game between the author and the reader. If you want to write a mystery, you must play by the rules. You want to fool your opponent, but you don't want to cheat. You must space your clues throughout, giving the reader a chance to solve the mystery before you reveal the answer at the end.

Another important ingredient in a mystery story is *danger* aimed at the character who is trying to solve the mystery. Often that character is a police detective or a private investigator— also known as a "private eye." Sometimes he or she is an amateur detective, someone who innocently stumbles into the middle of the plot.

Whether a professional or an amateur, the detective must follow the rules of the mystery game and use the clues hidden in the story. Finding those clues often leads to taking risks, and risks lead the detective into danger.

With danger comes *surprise.* A mystery leads readers to un-expected turns in the story. Often, a character the reader thinks is innocent turns out to be guilty. This surprise should be hinted at in a clue planted in the story, so when it happens later, the reader can either say, "Aha! I guessed that!" or "Oh, no! I missed that!"

Again, this must be done by the rules. The guilty character shouldn't be someone the reader doesn't see until the last page of the story. Readers want a fair chance to discover who is guilty by using the clues. In a way, the readers of mystery stories become amateur detectives themselves.

Another important element of any mystery is *motive*. Stories are believable only if there is a reason for the criminal to commit the crime. If the characters in the plot don't act logically, the whole story seems false. Whoever turns out to be guilty must have a clear purpose for his or her actions.

Setting is a big part of a mystery story. The setting, or background, describes where and when the action takes place. Mystery stories can happen anyplace on earth. They can be modern stories or they can be set hundreds of years ago. Some mystery stories even happen in the future.

The setting often tells readers what kind of mystery story this will be.

In the *cozy* mystery, the setting is gentle and refined, such as a beautiful home with seemingly kind people. The reader is lulled into a mood of peacefulness. However, the mood is broken by the discovery of a crime.

The *hardboiled detective* mystery is about as far away from a cozy mystery as a sunny garden is from a dark alley. The key word for a hardboiled detective mystery is "tough." The investigator, often a private detective, must deal with danger. There are many scenes of dramatic action. The setting is completely different from a cozy, too. In a hardboiled detective story, the setting is usually someplace where you wouldn't want to walk alone. The setting tells the reader: *Here lies danger.*

A *police procedural* is another kind of mystery. In it, the investigator is a police officer. The story includes a lot of police department rules, such as making sure the accused has been read his or her rights. A good police procedural takes readers into a working police station. Readers enjoy the specialized language and terms used by police officers investigating the crime.

In an *amateur detective* mystery, the investigator is someone who becomes involved in the plot by accident. Because he or she is an amateur, the detective in this type of story doesn't follow the same rules that apply to police or private investigators. The inexperience of the amateur allows him or her to break the rules. In this kind of story, the detective is usually someone with good common sense, and that quality helps him or her to find the clues and solve the mystery.

These four types of mysteries are the most widely found, but they are not the only kinds. There are nearly as many kinds of mystery stories as there are people who love reading them. Anyone can write one, including you. Decide when and where you want your story to take place, and what type of mystery you'd like to write. And remember some of these helpful ingredients: a *secret, riddle,* or *puzzle, clues, red herrings, danger, surprise, motive,* and *setting.*

People love reading mysteries because they're so much fun. Whether you like to read them or write them, a good mystery provides a great challenge. You will find plenty of challenges in the thirteen mystery stories in this collection. So turn the page and see how good you are at solving mysteries!

Ilana: In this story I was trying to say that if something frightening happens to you and you don't do something about it, you could grow up with nightmares.

Working with my dad was fun. We thought of lots of funny stuff. I hope my dad liked working on the story as much as I did. His personality was great and he had enough patience to fill twelve whales. I love my dad. I hope we do another story together. My father has encouraged me and now I know I can write a story.

Jonathan: "Matinee" is the easiest story I've ever written because Ilana is an astonishingly creative person and she did most of the work. I've always known Ilana is a born writer. When she was four years old, the preschool teacher asked all the class to dictate stories. Most were a sentence or two. Ilana's was five paragraphs long, detailed and beautifully crafted. But actually sitting down and writing with her was still amazing; without any formal training she knows how to plot, pace, and characterize. And she has a great sense of humor.

I love Ilana and swell with fatherly pride, but I think any person reading "Matinee" will agree that she's someone to look out for in the literary future.

MATINEE

BY JONATHAN KELLERMAN
AND ILANA KELLERMAN

"Be right back, Tori. I'm just going to get some popcorn."

"Uh-huh." Tori's eyes remained on the screen. The detective was searching the dark house, looking for the bloodthirsty killer. The music was scary. Emily wouldn't admit it, but popcorn was an excuse. She hated scary movies, but Tori loved them.

Emily made her way through the dark, empty theater. When she got to the lobby, the light hurt her eyes. The ceiling was painted with a mural. Chubby, smiling angels.

No one was working the counter. When she and Tori had come in, a tall, funny-looking boy with bad skin and big ears had watched them from behind the cash register. Now he was gone.

She went to the bathroom, washed her face, and looked at herself in the mirror. Straight red hair, the freckles she couldn't stand, big green eyes other people told her were beautiful. She thought they looked like traffic lights. Other people—grownups—also thought *she* was pretty, but no way. Her idea of pretty was Tori: curly black hair as shiny as licorice, blue eyes just the right size, and a perfect pink little mouth that always seemed to be smiling.

Emily dried her hands and went back to the snack bar. Now the funny-looking boy was there, wiping the counter. He was tall, as tall as a man, but awkward looking, like an overgrown child. Probably fourteen, three years older than Emily and Tori.

He was staring at her. His lower lip was shaking.

"Popcorn," she said. "And a Coke."

"Uh, medium or large?"

"Large, please."

The boy filled the cup. She thought his hands shook, too, but why would that be?

"Uh, butter or plain?"

"Butter. Lots of butter."

His look was so nervous, she found herself fighting back a giggle.

When he handed her back her change, his palm was moist.

Back on the screen, the detective was still looking for the killer. Emily made her way to her seat. As she sat down, some of the popcorn spilled on Tori's lap.

"Sorry, Tori."

No answer. Wow. Tori was really into the movie, thought Emily.

"Here, I got us some junk." Emily's hand brushed against Tori's leg. "Ooh, there's something sticky on you."

Silence.

"Tori?"

Emily touched her friend's shoulder. Tori's head slumped forward.

"Tori?"

Always joking, thought Emily. She moved closer and tapped Tori's back. Then she felt something sharp and pulled back. A wet dribble rolled down Emily's hand.

"Tori! Tori!"

Emily knew from the pain in her throat that she was screaming and screaming as loud as she could. But no one heard her because no one else was there. Up on the screen, the detective had found the murderer, and the two of them were fighting and struggling as the music swelled louder and louder and louder...

The doorbell rang, rescuing Emily from her nightmare. She was sweating and her heart was beating fast. The way it always did. The same memories, the same horrible pictures in her head.

It rang again and again, as if the person on the other side had been waiting a long time.

Emily finally got up, still feeling frightened.

She looked through the peephole. A tall, fine-looking young man stood out in the hallway. He wore a black suit, a white shirt, and a navy tie with maroon stripes. His smile was wide and friendly. His eyes were very brown.

"Yes?" said Emily through the door.

"Ms. Pierce?" Something white covered the peephole. It was a business card.

ROBERT CAMERON
LICENSED PRIVATE INVESTIGATOR
8765 SUNSET BOULEVARD
HOLLYWOOD, CALIFORNIA

"What can I do for you, Mr. Cameron?" asked Emily.

The card was removed and Cameron's handsome face came into view again.

"I was wondering if I could speak with you."

"About what?"

"Are you the same Emily Pierce who once lived in Paris Gulch, California?"

Emily gulped. "I—only for one summer and that was years ago."

"Nineteen years ago," said Cameron. His smile remained. A warm smile. Emily opened the door.

Cameron stood there with his hands in his pockets, grinning.

"Sorry to bother you at night. I came earlier, but you weren't here."

"I was working," said Emily, thinking of the worst job in the world—working as a pastry chef on the lunch shift at The TV Café, a snooty Beverly Hills restaurant. Then she thought about Paris Gulch and felt even worse.

"Nice apartment," said Cameron.

"Thanks—please, come in."

She offered him a chair and coffee.

"No, thanks," he said, pulling out a small notebook.

Emily sat down. "What do you want to talk to me about?"

Cameron hesitated, as if he really didn't want to talk about it. "Things that happened nineteen years ago. A distant cousin of yours named Victoria Tamberlyn."

Emily thought she was going to faint. "I called her Tori," she heard herself saying. "Everyone did."

"I'm sorry," said Cameron. He offered her a tissue and she realized she was crying.

She wiped her eyes. "I went to the movies with her. Every day that summer, until…"

Cameron let her cry for a while. Then he said, "I know this is hard, but someone hired me to find out who murdered her."

"Who?" asked Emily.

"Family members," said Cameron. "I'm sorry, I can't tell you more. Detectives have to keep everything confidential."

"Have you found any clues?"

Cameron turned the pages of his notebook. "What I know is this: Nineteen years ago, Tori Tamberlyn was eleven years old and living in Paris Gulch, where her father owned the biggest business in town."

"Paris Gulch Oil," said Emily. "Mr. Tamberlyn had dozens and dozens of oil wells just outside town."

"The town depended upon the oil," said Cameron. "Right after Tori's murder, the wells closed down and so did everything else."

"I didn't know," said Emily. "How sad."

"How did you come to be there that summer?"

"My parents had a very rough divorce and neither of them could take care of me for a couple of months. Tori's mom and my dad were third cousins. Tori and I were the same age, and someone thought it would be a good idea for me to live with her family."

"Was it?"

"Yes. Until Tori was…" Emily stopped herself and choked back tears. Cameron's eyes were soft and friendly.

"The summer was wonderful," she said. "Tori was wonderful. We didn't know each other, but when we found out we were cousins, we were so happy. And not only were we cousins, we became best friends. We did everything together. Rode bikes, hiked around the desert, played with Tori's dog—Sparkly—and told stories. We also went to the movies nearly every day. The twelve o'clock matinee."

Sweat was pouring down Emily's back. She hid her face and muttered, "That was where it happened."

She felt a strong hand on her shoulder.

"It's okay," said Cameron. "Sometimes talking about it helps."

"Not me," said Emily. "It just hurts."

Cameron didn't say anything for a few moments. Then he gave a soft smile. "Are you hungry? I've been working all day and haven't eaten a bite."

"Me too," said Emily, discovering she *was* hungry. "I can fix something for you."

"I was thinking more of having dinner out," said Cameron. "On my way over I noticed a pretty little Italian place down the block. Giamante's."

"Yes, they've got great pasta."

"Would you like to join me tonight?"

"Yes," she heard herself saying. She felt her heart quicken. But not from fear.

They walked to the restaurant. The sun was setting and the city sky was purple and orange. As they entered Giamante's, Emily noticed a dirty-looking, scratched gray car by the curb. Its engine was running. The man at the wheel seemed to be staring at her.

As she looked at him, she noticed that he had bad skin and big ears. Just like the boy at the matinee's snack counter, years ago. But how could that be? The man looked at her and she shivered as he pulled away.

"What's the matter?" asked Bob Cameron, holding the door open for her.

"Oh, nothing. Let's eat. I'm starving."

The food was delicious and Bob was sweet. He talked about his work without giving many details. He had once been a policeman and loved being a private eye. Emily talked about herself: her job, her hobby—telling stories to children in the hospital—growing up without a family. Then she found herself returning to that summer. The summer with Tori.

"I really miss her!" she admitted. "Sometimes I still think about her and cry. Do you really think you can ever find out who did it?"

"I'll try my best," answered Bob.

"Do you have any suspects?"

"Not yet. Do you?"

"The theater was empty. Just Tori and me. And a funny-looking boy who worked at the popcorn counter."

"Jack Lawrenson," said Bob. "Actually, I looked into him because his name came up in the police reports and he's got a criminal record."

"Really! What did he do?"

"Lots of things."

"What?"

"Robbery, assault—let's just say he's not a guy you'd like to have dinner with."

"But I—"

"What?"

"I can't be sure, but as we walked in, I thought I saw someone who looked like him."

"What do you mean?" said Bob. "That was nineteen years ago."

"Yes, but Jack Lawrenson had certain features—pimples, gigantic ears—and this man did, too."

Bob grew serious. "Where'd you see this guy?"

"Right by the curb as we came in," said Emily.

He got up to look, but Emily said, "He's gone now."

Bob sat back down. "I'm sure it's nothing." But his eyes looked concerned.

The waiter brought dessert.

As they finished, Bob said, "This is hard to say, Emily, but Tori's family has been sad for so long. They really want to find out what happened and maybe you can help."

"How?"

"By going to Paris Gulch. Maybe being there can help you remember something."

"I thought that after Tori's father shut down the oil wells

everything disappeared."

"Yes," said Bob. "There's not much left. But the theater's still there."

Emily hesitated. Her heart was beating loudly and there was a lump in her throat. All these years, she'd wanted to know who the killer was, too. But she remembered nothing. How could going back help?

Bob put his hand on hers. His eyes were kind. "I'm sorry, forget it. It's too much to ask."

"No," said Emily. "I'll go. Why not?"

That night the dreams came back. But worse: clearer, brighter, louder, faster. More *real*.

Emily woke up sweating at five-thirty in the morning. Her hands were cold as ice. Her legs felt heavy, as if made of stone. She lay in bed, trying not to think of the murder. Or what she'd agreed to do. Then she thought of Bob protecting her and she felt better.

He picked her up at nine o'clock and handed her a cup of coffee and a doughnut. She'd already made coffee and the two of them laughed. They got in his car and headed for the highway.

"It's a three-hour drive," said Bob, "if we don't hit bad traffic."

Three hours, thought Emily. In all these years, she'd never found the time.

As they left the city and entered the desert, the air got hotter. At first they passed through small towns. Once it seemed as if a gray car was following them, but when Emily turned to look, it was gone. After that, each time she saw any gray vehicle, she swung her head and stared. No sign of the big-eared man. She was being silly.

Bob turned off the highway and on to a narrow, bumpy road. The sun was beating down and the sand was yellowish. All Emily saw from the car was sand. So much sand. Then a few cactus plants and a scattering of rocks.

They drove a bit more. Suddenly, she saw it.

Where buildings had once stood, there were now piles of old wood, crumbling and dusty and brown. Spider webs stretched across sagging doorways. Emily saw half a sign hanging over a broken window:

Munk and Junk. The candy store. Tori's favorite place to hang out after the matinee.

This empty, dirty strip had once been Oakmore Street.

Bob stopped and parked the car. As Emily got out, she tripped over something and fell, skinning her knee, which began to bleed.

Bob rushed over and put a napkin on the scrape. Blood leaked through the paper.

"I'm okay," Emily said.

"Are you sure?"

"Yes." She looked down and saw the thing that had tripped her. An old, fossilized bone—a skull, white and cracked.

Probably a cow or a horse.

Bob kicked it away.

Emily's knee had stopped bleeding, and as she got up, she noticed how silent it was.

Bob helped her up and looked toward the top of Oakmore Street. The largest of the woodpiles stood there. Almost a building. Four walls and a roof, but something was missing.

The marquee in front. The big, bright marquee that had once been full of shiny black letters and surrounded by shiny bulbs.

The only light now came from the sun, straight above.

Twelve o'clock noon.

"Matinee time," said Bob, and he took her hand.

The door was still attached by one hinge. Bob pulled it and it creaked.

Still holding Emily's hand, he drew her inside.

The door closed creakily. Bob stopped and looked around the dark, grimy lobby.

There were holes in the roof that let in just a little light.

The floor beneath them sagged and seemed to give way under their weight.

"Wait," said Bob. "I'd better check to make sure everything's safe."

"Okay," said Emily, but her voice was shaky.

Bob took her hand again and gave it a gentle squeeze.

"I'll just be a minute—will you be all right?"

"Sure."

He went farther into the old theater and soon the darkness swallowed him up.

Emily stood there, listening to his footsteps. Then they, too, disappeared.

Silence.

Not even the beat of her heart. Because it wasn't racing. She didn't feel frightened.

Just the opposite. She felt calm. Peaceful. No, not peaceful. Dreamlike.

She stepped forward. In front of her was a rusted metal frame and some pieces of broken glass.

The old popcorn counter.

She remembered the boy's face again. The big ears and bad skin. Jack Lawrenson. The way he'd looked at her...She'd asked for popcorn and he'd struggled while filling the container. His hands had been shaking and his pimply face had been sweating. What had he been so nervous about? Had he killed Tori? And if so, why?

She stood there in the empty, rotting lobby, trying to remember more. But nothing came. The mural had faded. Too dark to see much of the chubby angels.

Suddenly she felt alone. Bob had been away for too long.

She went into the theater.

It was so dark, she felt as if she were falling into a black hole. She could see outlines and shadows...the same sloping floor, but no screen, just a big, empty space. Emily found herself remembering the movie that day. The detective chasing the killer.

She reached out to take hold of a seat and felt nothing. There were chairs—but not rows of them, just a few broken-down wrecks. The leather had worn off and the wooden frames sagged.

She walked slowly.

Toward the row where she and Tori had sat.

The same two chairs, both ruined. But Tori's still had some leather. And a jagged rip.

She came closer, felt dizzy, and lost her balance. Her arm shot out and her fingers found their place.

On the rip.

The leather felt stiff and cracked and cold.

Then something even colder touched her.

From behind.

Hands choking her, cutting off her air. She reached back to pry them loose, but they were too strong and the pressure grew stronger, forcing her down.

She struggled, hearing hard breathing at her neck. Someone working hard. At killing her.

She tried to fight but felt herself grow weak. Then, an even greater darkness...total black...

Then screams, thunder.

The hands around her neck shook. Then they loosened.

Emily collapsed.

She awoke to see the painted ceiling in the theater. Faded, chubby angels. But she could make out the details. The big room was lighter.

Then a face loomed above her.

Big ears, bad skin.

She started to scream, and a big hand came down and patted her shoulder.

"It's okay, miss."

"Please! Don't *hurt* me!"

The big hand withdrew. The eyes in the homely face were gentle, like a dog's.

Emily started to shake and cry.

The big hand showed her something. A police badge.

Detective Jack Lawrenson. Homicide.

The second badge she'd seen in two days—where was *Bob?* She called out his name.

Lawrenson smiled down at her. "Don't worry about him, miss. We've got him in custody."

Emily sat up and saw Bob in handcuffs, held by two uniformed policemen.

He saw her and his eyes narrowed. "It's not over!" he screamed. "I'll get you—"

Lawrenson barked an order, and the policemen dragged Bob away, kicking and screaming.

"I don't understand," said Emily. "He said he was…"

"He's a bad guy," said Lawrenson. "Spent most of his life in jail. He came back to kill you."

"But why?"

"Two classic reasons, miss. Revenge and money."

"Revenge for what?" said Emily.

"He thought Albert Tamberlyn—Victoria's father—ruined

his father, Robert Cameron, Senior. Cameron and Tamberlyn were partners in the oil company, but Cameron gambled away his fortune and sold his share to Tamberlyn. Then, when he lost that, too, he began blaming Tamberlyn. He died poor, and his son grew up rough. Bob Junior started with boyish pranks, but he moved on to crime pretty fast."

"Did he kill Tori—no, he couldn't have, he was just a kid."

Lawrenson's blue eyes grew sad and he nodded.

"A kid killing a kid?" said Emily.

"Like I said, he moved on to bad stuff pretty fast. Sneaking into theaters was the least of his problems. We know he was the murderer because he bragged about it to a cellmate in prison. He's killed other people, too."

"Oh, no," said Emily.

"I'm sorry," said Lawrenson, and he reached out to touch her again but stopped himself. "He always liked knives. Even while in prison, he killed a man. We think he's been planning to kill you for years."

"Why?"

"He's gotten the crazy idea that there's still oil here, and as his father's descendant he can claim this old town once you're gone."

"What do I have to do with it?"

"You don't know?" asked Lawrenson.

Emily shook her head.

"Not only were you and Tori best friends, you were cousins, right?"

"Just distant cousins," said Emily. "Before that summer I

never even knew her."

"But you're still her closest living relative, miss. Tori's father left the town to you. You own Paris Gulch." Lawrenson winked. "And who knows, maybe there *is* oil."

"This is all too much," said Emily.

Lawrenson smiled again. "At least you're safe and alive. And this time Cameron should be going away for life."

Emily started to stand. Her knees felt weak.

"Here, let me help you, miss."

"Call me Emily," she said.

"Okay," he said. "If you call me Jack."

She took his arm and they walked out into the sunlight. He was still smiling, but not like a rescuing hero.

More like a little boy. A shy one. A boy trying to hide his feelings but not doing a very good job of it.

When she looked up at him, he blushed.

Suddenly she knew why he'd been so nervous that day when she'd come out to the snack counter for popcorn.

That made her smile, too.

Joan: I invited Nicole, my teenage granddaughter, to co-author a story with me because she has always loved to write, and she loves to read mysteries. We began our collaboration through phone calls, because Nicole lives in Fort Collins, Colorado, and I live in Houston, Texas.

Nicole: Our story really started when Grandma sent a letter with two ideas and asked if either of them interested me. We both got excited about the same idea, so we began brainstorming over the phone.

Joan: By the time Nicole came for a summer visit, we had developed our story and found our main character. Next, we thought up our suspects, gave them names and descriptions, and chose our setting.

Nicole: When we began writing the story on Grandma's computer, we first had to come up with a good opening sentence. After that, the rest of the story began to fall into place.

Joan: We worked well together. Often, I'd start a sentence and Nicole would finish it. We thought in the same pattern.

Nicole: It was a lot of fun to write this story together. I hope we can do it again.

Joan Lowery Nixon   Nicole Marie Brush

THE DISAPPEARANCE OF GAVIN McCANN

BY JOAN LOWERY NIXON
AND NICOLE MARIE BRUSH

Gavin McCann told me his house was haunted—haunted by his sister Zetta and her husband, Henry Walbanks. I always thought haunted houses had ghosts, but Gavin said that visitors who refuse to go home are even scarier.

It was their arguments that scared me. I live next door, and even in my house I could hear the Walbankses shouting at Gavin. Henry Walbanks always wanted money. He kept investing in one business after another, and all of them failed.

Gavin never shouted back, even though he told me he got tired of giving money to Mr. Walbanks. Gavin was the kindest, happiest, most gentle person I had ever met. Even though he was sixty-seven and I was twelve, we were good friends, which is why I call him Gavin.

When I first met Carrie Blackwood, my best friend, she said, "Wow, Elizabeth! You live next door to Gavin McCann, the famous artist? Cool!"

I thought it was cool, too. His house and ours are on what I think is the prettiest street in Pinedale, Colorado, because it has a spectacular view of the Rockies.

Everybody's seen Gavin's drawings in their favorite magazines. He's famous for his "Can You Find It?" pictures, in which objects, animals, or faces are hidden within a mass of squiggles. His drawings for kids' magazines are kind of easy, but the ones he draws for grownups can get tricky and hard to figure out.

That's where I come in. I love deciphering all kinds of things—puzzles, math problems, and mysteries. So Gavin sometimes asks me to come over and see if I can decipher his really hard drawings.

I had helped him with a series of drawings just the evening before we discovered he was missing.

It was about eleven-thirty in the morning, and Carrie had brought over another armload of mystery novels. I heard Mrs. Walbanks screaming and shouting, so Mom, Carrie, and I rushed across the lawn to see what was going on.

Mrs. Walbanks, a tall, heavyset woman with bleached blond hair, grabbed Mom by the shoulders and yelled, "Where's Gavin? Where's my brother gone?"

It took Mom several minutes to calm Mrs. Walbanks down enough to hear her story. Mrs. Walbanks said she thought Gavin had been sleeping late, but when she went to check, she discovered that his bed hadn't been slept in.

I was scared. I didn't want anything bad to happen to Gavin.

"Have you called the police?" Mom asked.

"No," Mrs. Walbanks answered, and she shook her head so hard that I thought her false teeth would fly out. "Do you really think I should call them?"

"She's weird," I whispered to Carrie. "Calling the police ought to be the first thing anybody would think of."

"Right!" Carrie whispered back.

I asked Mrs. Walbanks, "Did Gavin pack any clothes? Is his suitcase missing? Did you check his calendar to see if he had a meeting out of town?"

She gave me a "Why don't you mind your own business" look, and I wondered how upset she really was about the disappearance of her brother.

"Why don't you go and play, little girl?" she said with a scowl.

I wasn't about to leave, because I had begun to suspect that she might have had something to do with Gavin's disappearance.

"Mom," I said, "Gavin's all right, isn't he?"

"I'm sure he is," she said. Mom patted my shoulder and led Mrs. Walbanks inside her brother's house. Carrie and I followed.

Gavin's house contained a collection of things he loved, and nothing matched, which drove his sister crazy. This was just one more thing she nagged him about.

In the living room sat a fat, overstuffed sofa, with a fat, overstuffed Mr. Walbanks plopped down in the middle of it. He didn't seem to be worried about his missing brother-in-law. His attention was on a TV cartoon and his can of beer.

Gavin's short, plump housekeeper, Shirley Shiner, vacuumed around Mr. Walbanks, sighing self-pityingly as usual. At least she didn't grumble, as she often did, that life is hard and the world is unfair. She didn't even look up as we came in.

"Use the phone in Gavin's studio, Mom," I said. "It's quieter in there."

"Right," Carrie said.

The studio looked as it always did, with stacks of paper and art piled everywhere. Against the wall were Gavin's files, where he kept the originals of his drawings. He told me that a local art dealer, Paul Roman, had offered over and over to buy them, but Gavin's dream was to someday present his collection to his university.

Money didn't mean much to Gavin. His clothes were like his house—mismatched, sloppy, and usually stained with ink. He loved his work and enjoyed making people happy. Funny though, he didn't like to socialize, and sometimes even living in small, quiet Pinedale got to be too much for him.

As Mom called the police, Mrs. Shiner appeared in the doorway. She gave a long sigh and said, "I gotta clean in here now."

"I don't think you should clean the office," I said. "Not until the police say you can."

"Right," Carrie said.

We've read enough mystery stories to know that the scene of the crime has to be left as it is. We weren't actually sure this was the scene of the crime. We didn't know yet if there even *was* a crime. But it was important not to mess things up any more than they already were before the police arrived.

Mrs. Shiner looked a little startled, then a little scared, and vanished from the doorway.

"What's the matter with her?" I whispered to Carrie.

I walked behind the slant-top table where Gavin does most of his work, expecting to see his latest drawing, but instead there was a large manila envelope with ELIZABETH written on it in big black lettering.

"Hey, look!" I said. "This is for me."

"Yeah, right," Carrie said.

I reached for it, but Mrs. Walbanks was faster. She snatched it up, opened it, and pulled out a single sheet with a complicated Gavin McCann drawing on it.

I didn't even have a chance to get a good look at the drawing before she popped it back inside the envelope and tucked it under her arm. She turned to Mom. "I don't want to remove anything from my brother's office until he returns," she snapped.

Mom nodded in agreement and said to me, "It's probably a good idea, Elizabeth."

"Could I at least see what's in the envelope?" I asked.

"No," Mrs. Walbanks said. "What if your fingers aren't clean? What if you smear it?"

I didn't argue, but I definitely didn't agree. If Gavin wanted me to have the drawing, then I should at least be able to see it. I'd have to figure out a way.

Within a few minutes a detective arrived and introduced himself as Mark Sanders. He'd heard of Gavin McCann, of course, and he asked a million questions. Afterward, he inspected the house thoroughly and said he could find no evidence of foul play.

"Does that mean that someone Gavin knew and trusted could have lured him out of the house?" I gulped. "And maybe *murdered* him?"

Everybody stared at me, even Carrie. I felt a little sick because I didn't want to think of something that awful happening to Gavin.

"Now, Elizabeth," Mom said. "You've been reading too many mystery novels." She smiled at Detective Sanders. "Elizabeth and Carrie have a mystery reading club."

Detective Sanders studied me. "Do you have any information that might make us think Mr. McCann's disappearance was the result of murder?"

I glanced at Mrs. Walbanks, who was still scowling at me. I didn't want to be next on her list. "Not really," I answered.

"Right," Carrie said.

Mrs. Walbanks grabbed Mom's arm and tugged her toward the door. "Thanks for your help," she said. "Detective Sanders will take care of things now."

As we left, I glanced again at the envelope under her arm. Gavin had meant that for me, and I was determined to get my hands on it.

Carrie's mom called and she had to go home, but I kept an eye on Gavin's house. As soon as I saw Detective Sanders leave, I walked around to the back door and turned the knob. Just as I figured, with Mrs. Shiner still there, the back door was unlocked, and I quietly let myself in. I not only had some investigating of my own to do, I wanted my envelope. Mrs. Walbanks had no right to keep it from me.

I tiptoed down the hallway to Gavin's studio and stepped inside the room. There was my envelope, with ELIZABETH on it, lying on the art table, halfway across the room.

I took a step toward it when Mrs. Walbanks's voice rang out, and I froze. "Henry!" she yelled. "Someone's been in these files! Some of the file folders are empty! The drawings are gone!"

Mrs. Walbanks was kneeling on the studio floor, her back to me, her head practically inside one of the drawers to the file. She hadn't seen or heard me.

I moved a step closer to my envelope.

Henry shouted back from the sofa, where he seemed to be permanently planted, "Keep looking! It means money in the bank for us! Those drawings are valuable!"

Inch by inch I moved toward the envelope, but before I could grab it, Mrs. Walbanks's head popped out of the file drawer. She saw me.

"Get out of here!" she yelled, and leaped for the envelope. I never saw anybody move so fast. "Henry!" she screeched. "C'mere and help me! This kid is trying to get her hands on one of the pictures."

I wasn't sure what Henry might do—if he was even *able* to move—so I made a break for it. I rushed into the hall, out the back door, and straight into Mrs. Shiner, who was leaving for the day. Her hat flew off, and her shopping bag fell from her hand.

"I'm sorry!" I cried, and tried to shove her things back into the shopping bag—apron, handbag, flat-heeled shoes, and a folder from which some papers had spilled.

"Go away! Leave me alone! I don't need your help!" Mrs. Shiner nervously snatched the folder from my hands, shoving the papers back inside. I was sure I'd caught a glimpse of one of Gavin's drawings. At least I thought I was sure.

I couldn't take the folder from her, but I had to find out what was going on.

"I'm sorry," I said again, and headed for my house.

As soon as she was far enough away, I followed her, making sure she didn't see me. She walked four long blocks to the main shopping street of Pinedale and entered a soda shop.

I could see clearly through the window. I didn't go inside. I thought it was safer.

Mrs. Shiner plopped down at a corner table, where a tall, well-dressed dark-haired man was eating. She ordered something. When the waitress left, I saw Mrs. Shiner pull the folder from her shopping bag and hand it to her companion. He glanced inside, then quickly slipped her an envelope.

Was this a payoff? Carrie and I had read about payoffs in our mystery novels.

I stepped into a nearby phone booth and called Carrie, quickly telling her where I was. "Come on! Hurry!" I said. "We've got a crime taking place."

"Right," Carrie said.

She showed up just before Mrs. Shiner left the shop and waddled down the street. We decided to let her go and follow the folder to see where it led us.

It wasn't far. Just a few doors down the street, the dark-haired man entered an office building. We watched the numbers on the elevator as he rode it to the fifth floor.

The directory listed only a few names for the fifth floor: Thaddeus Gridley, dentist; Emily Johnson, attorney-at-law; and Paul Roman, art dealer.

"Paul Roman!" I turned to Carrie. "We need to talk to Detective Sanders."

"Oh, right," Carrie said.

We raced to Pinedale's police station, over on the next block, and asked for Detective Sanders.

He had just come in, so he took us into his office, where I poured out everything I'd seen and heard.

Detective Sanders gave me a questioning look. "How does all this fit together?" he asked. "You've told me about an alleged art theft involving Mrs. Shiner and Paul Roman, and you suspect Gavin McCann's sister and brother-in-law of arranging his disappearance in order to lay claim to his drawings."

"Why does it all have to fit together?" I said. "The way I see it, there are two crimes: art theft and"—I gulped— "murder."

He frowned at me. "Your mother told me you girls read too many mystery novels," he said. "I think she may be right."

"Look," I insisted. "I can prove what I told you. If you visit Paul Roman's office before he has a chance to sell the drawings, you'll find them."

Detective Sanders nodded. "That will take a search warrant, which can be arranged. However, the conversation you overheard between the Walbankses is only hearsay."

I bounced eagerly in my chair. "I think that the answer to

Gavin's disappearance is in the envelope he left for me. Mrs. Walbanks wouldn't give it to me because she said it was valuable. But I wouldn't be surprised if Gavin knew he was in danger and named his murderers."

"Oh, wow! Right!" Carrie said.

Detective Sanders made a quick phone call and said to us, "I've sent someone to talk to Paul Roman." He shoved back his chair and got to his feet. "Let's visit the Walbankses and take a look at that envelope. Come on. I'll give you a lift."

When we arrived at the house, Mrs. Walbanks wasn't very happy to see us, and she really looked pained when Detective Sanders asked for my envelope.

"I don't see any reason to show you that envelope or *any* of Gavin's drawings," she said, and her husband grunted his agreement from the sofa in the living room.

"If you'd prefer, I'll get a search warrant," Detective Sanders said firmly.

I wanted to cheer. I could tell that he was getting really interested in the case.

Her hands fluttering nervously, Mrs. Walbanks handed over the envelope. Detective Sanders opened it, pulled out a single drawing, and examined it, turning it over and over.

"What are these squiggles?" he asked. "I don't understand this picture at all."

I eagerly reached for the drawing and began to study it. Piece by piece, the drawing began to come alive. In the left corner, nestled in tree branches, I made out the profiles of Zetta and Henry Walbanks. The leaves around them turned into dollar bills and a fat, overstuffed sofa.

"The suspects!" I said aloud. "They're here!"

Detective Sanders and Carrie peered over my shoulder as I pointed out the drawing of the Walbankses.

"I'll be darned," Detective Sanders said. "I see them. What else have you found?"

Moving from left to right, I discovered a bus, a mountain, and a tombstone. "Murder!" I cried.

But this was not Gavin's tombstone. Written on it were words that I could just make out: PEACE AND QUIET.

"Murder?" Detective Sanders repeated. He took a step toward Mrs. Walbanks, who turned as white as the paper the drawing was on.

And then I started to laugh. I laughed so hard, I fell to the rug and held my stomach.

"It's not murder," I told Detective Sanders. Ignoring the amazed expressions on everyone's faces, I got up, tugged him and Carrie outside, and said, "Let's go wrap up the art theft."

"Do you want to tell me what's so funny about a suspected murder?" he asked.

"I told you. It wasn't murder. Gavin showed me where he's hiding from his sister and her husband." I pointed to the lower right-hand side of the picture and helped him see that among the squiggles was something that looked like a rustic mountain cabin, with Gavin's face smiling from the window.

"I think your mother's wrong about those mystery stories," Detective Sanders said. "When you can quickly solve a case, as you've just done, it's obvious that you *don't* read too many.

You've read just enough."

Carrie and I grinned at each other. "We not only read my teries," I told him, "someday we might even..."

"Write them," Carrie said.

Annie A. Anderson, age twelve, lives across the street from Carole Nelson Douglas in Fort Worth, Texas. The home-schooled daughter of educators Bill and LeVonna Anderson, she is a fan of Carole's Midnight Louie—a hairy-chested, hardboiled feline sleuth in Las Vegas, who narrates Carole's mystery series of the same name.

Although Annie has had many exotic pets in her life, she has never had a cat. "There's always a hamster out," she notes. For this collection, Annie concocted a scenario with Louie as a fish out of water, so to speak, in the desert. The Anderson family rescued an abandoned newborn pup, Bear, before Christmas 1993, so Annie wanted this sur-vivor—and a jewel thief and a movie—in Louie's tale, too. Carole then corralled these elements within the limits of a short story.

Midnight Louie's role, as always, was to provide narra-tive sass and class. Louie was pretty unhappy about giving an in*fur*ior species—dogs—leading roles, but behaved so generously to creatures not of his own kind that he even got the Anderson iguana into the story...in Louie's own inimitable way.

Carole Nelson Douglas   *Annie A. Anderson*

Midnight Louie, Esq.

DOG COLLAR

BY CAROLE NELSON DOUGLAS
AND ANNIE A. ANDERSON

They say to let sleeping dogs lie. I am in full agreement with them, whoever "they" are.

Dogs are naturally a "lying" breed anyway—grinning, bootlicking curs who will pretend to be man's best friend while snarfing the last morsel of overlooked salami from his trouser cuff.

Besides, even when dogs are just lying down, they are generally sleeping. And when they are sleeping, they are not barking, or chewing on their owner's best sneakers, or chasing yours truly and others of my kind.

What am I? you may wonder. First of all, the name is Louie. Midnight Louie. I am twenty pounds of street-smart muscle and bone in a sleek jet-black overcoat. Some call me a private detective, others a lazy layabout, although the layabout part is merely a disguise. Mostly, around this town, I am known as one tough dude and all-around cool cat. "This town" is not just any-old-where either.

I am Las Vegas born and fed. You know Las Vegas: that Fourth-of-July sparkler of a city in the Nevada desert, where big folks go to eat buffets and play games of chance, and littler folks go to see pirate ships and pyramids and take live-action rides that would make Indiana Jones lose his cookies, not to mention his salami.

But where there are fun and games, glitz and glamour, and cash and coins, there are people who want to get the loot without working for it.

That is where I come in. I am Las Vegas's perfect undercover operative. I am hush-puppy soft on my tootsies and smarter than the previously mentioned Mr. Jones's whip. While I am usually a pussycat with my pals, I can be a tiger on your tail if you do something against the law.

At the moment I am off duty, relaxing in a dressing room at the Goliath, the biggest and gaudiest hotel-casino in Las Vegas. I am quite a pet among showgirls in this town, those skyscraper-tall ladies who wear rhinestones and feathers onstage.

In fact, I am resting on a red velvet pillow next to Miss Mitzi Malone, a semi-star of the show who has been chosen to make a dramatic entrance in tonight's last act.

She is a kindly lady with lots of hair dyed an odd salmon-pink (yum-yum) color and false fingernails long enough to pick a safe. Despite these shivs, she is able to interrupt her makeup ritual to pat my head now and again.

Unfortunately, we are not alone. On her other side, in a canvas carrier, is one of the earlier mentioned abominations: a dog. Well, I think that it is a dog. It is fresh from the beauty parlor and smells like air freshener. It has a salmon-pink permanent wave all over its little body, which is shaved here and there so the critter resembles a chenille bedspread. It must weigh a whole six pounds after Thanksgiving dinner. It goes by

the name of Ritzi and speaks in high, sharp barks that would make a stone deaf.

Though this poodle Ritzi is a bit of a dim bulb in the noodle, it is the light of Miss Mitzi's life and goes with her everywhere. At least it is asleep now, curled into a ball the size of a large salmon-pink powder puff. Ick! I wonder if it is at least eatable?

I open one emerald-green eye at the arrival of Miss Mitzi's gentleman caller, a lowbrow type around town known as Lennie the Ferret. If only he were as classy as a ferret.

"Oh, Lennie," Miss Mitzi squeals in greeting. Sometimes she actually sounds like Ritzi. "Tonight I will wear the fabulous Czarina's diamond necklace onstage. This is my moment to shine."

"Sure, doll," he says, glancing at a handsome black velvet box on the makeup counter between Miss Mitzi and me. The box has a soft sheen much like my own formal coat. When they want understated elegance, they always go for black velvet.

"I saw the armed guard outside," Lennie adds. "Good thing he knows me. Let me slip this little gem on for you."

While Miss Mitzi sweeps up her salmon-pink hair and bends her head forward, Mr. Lennie the Ferret opens the black velvet box and pulls out a fistful of glittering diamonds. Then that fist and the necklace go into his right jacket pocket while his left hand slips into his left pocket. He pulls out an identical fistful of glittering ice. Before Miss Mitzi can blink, Mr. Lennie is leashing a copy, not the real necklace, around her dainty throat.

But before Mr. Lennie the Ferret can blink, I am extending

an agile paw. I hook a claw into his right jacket pocket, snagging the gems and pulling them into full view.

Miss Mitzi frowns as my motion catches her eye. She stares at the diamonds Mr. Lennie the Ferret is fastening around her neck, then her mouth opens in a big "O."

"What is that?" She points at the loot now hanging from my mitt. "Lennie! You...thief! You switched rhinestones for the Czarina's necklace. I thought you loved me."

"Sure, sure," he says, snatching the diamonds from my grasp. "Almost as much as you love this mutt here."

At that he grabs Ritzi's carrier and zips it shut. The wimpy teacup poodle awakens with a mousy squeak, which Miss Mitzi echoes in heart-wrenching tones.

"Do the act and keep your mouth shut," he tells her, "or little Miss Ritzi is history."

Big Miss Mitzi claps one hand on her rhinestone-swathed throat and another over her open mouth. If my shivs were as long as hers, I would stab the guy, but she is too shocked to do anything but wail.

I am shocked, too, but I know what I must do: tail, not wail.

Midnight Louie is on the case!

I am off my cushy seat and onto the floor. Nobody notices me. Not the crook on his way out, nor the armed guard, who sees nothing wrong with Miss Mitzi's boyfriend taking her dog for a walk.

Luckily, it is my favorite time outside, night. I follow Lennie and the yipping yapper into the pitch-dark parking lot. When he dumps Ritzi's carrier in the trunk of a dusty black Ford, I am the swift black shadow that jumps up and slips into a corner, careful to keep my tail clear of the slamming trunk lid.

Bang. Here we are, alone at last, me and a dog the color of pink lemonade. I tell the victim to calm down, that I am here and all is well. But Ritzi keeps making like a crybaby during the long, bouncing ride in complete darkness to wherever Lennie is going.

When we arrive, he pulls the carrier from the trunk, springing me without knowing it. I dash under the car to get my bearings. First of all, I am standing in the world's biggest sandbox, for which I have no use at all at the moment. I can smell creosote bushes in the distance. A cactus needle is dueling one of my front fingernails.

After my look-see, I am not happy. We are in the middle of the Big Lonesome, the desert that surrounds Las Vegas. Why would a diamond thief hightail it to the desert? Certainly not to send his loot out of town via UPS. More likely to send it via California condor.

While I ponder the whys and wherefores, I suddenly hear Mr. Lennie in conversation with someone. Unless he has taken up talking to Ritzi, which I highly doubt, he is meeting an accomplice.

I edge out from under a tire to peek. Sure enough, two sets of legs stand in the moonlit sand, with Ritzi's carrier dumped between them.

"What's with the dog?" the new man asks.

"Insurance," Lennie growls. (See what I mean? Being around dogs can debase even someone as low as Lennie.) "You know what to do with the stuff?" I hear a brittle clink, like glasses chiming together. The necklace is on the move.

"It's a wrap," the guy says with a funny laugh, like he is making a joke only Lennie would get. "It'll reach L.A. pronto, with no questions asked."

"Fine," says Lennie. "I'll head there now. You better deliver."

"I will. Hey, what about the dog?"

"Leave it for the buzzards," Lennie shouts back. "It's a witness."

I am surprised to hear an engine turn over; my sheltering tire starts spinning in the sand. Luckily, it stalls for a second, or I would be as flat as the coyote in a Roadrunner cartoon.

I manage to duck as the car revs away. A pair of small red tail-lights glare at me for a long time. The other man is gone, though I heard no other car. All I hear now is Ritzi whimpering. For once the pooch is right: this situation is something to whine about. Here we are, dozens of miles out in the desert, in the dark, with no way home.

My first problem is springing the pooch. I look over the canvas carrier, pleased to discover it opens with a zipper. I am a past master of zippers. The zipper's metal pull-tab always has a nice little hole in it, just made for my front saber-tooth. All I have to do is anchor the bag by putting my full fighting weight on the bottom—"Quiet, pipsqueak!"—then impale my tooth in the tab hole, and jerk my head, taking the zipper along for the ride.

After a few minutes' struggle, I am rewarded when Ritzi springs to freedom and begins lathering my face with a rubbery wet tongue. Yuck. Poison dog lips, as others have observed before.

"Calm down, kid," I tell her. "And cut out the jumping. You are ruffling my only dress suit and your little nails are like knives. Also, save the saliva. In this desert, you will need it. We had better start hoofing it somewhere, because when the sun rises we will be hot, thirsty, and twenty hours away from Doomsville unless we find civilization. So come along and behave yourself."

Nothing can dampen Ritzi's spirits now that she is free. "Oh, Mr. Midnight, thank you for saving me from the buzzards! I will follow you anywhere."

That is a dog for you, eternally grateful from the git-go. You have got to admire their optimism.

"Listen, kid," I say. "Does that cute little sniffer of yours actually work? Mine is a superior model, but I do best following a seafood trail, of which there is darn little in this desert. Did you perchance pick up some scent on the shoe of the dude who came to talk to your abductor?"

"As a matter of fact," Ritzi says with a prissy sniff, "I did detect an awful odor I have been trying to ignore."

"Do not ignore it. Follow that scent. By the way, what is it?"

"I believe it is a low form of lizard leaving."

So we hoof it through the night, following the snuffling sounds of Ritzi's itsy-bitsy black nose, on the trail of iguana guano. (This guano is usually the dropping of bats, but I figure lizard leavings are similar.)

Speaking of creepy things, I keep a lookout for snakes, spiders the size of baseballs, and other dangerous fellow travelers.

The sunrise is real pretty, but it shows miles of nowhere and nothing, all sand-brown. Ritzi's dye-job coat stands out like a neon sign, but nobody is looking for one out here. Nobody is looking for us. If we are to save our bacon, or our salami, we will have to do the looking. We will have to find somebody.

Who would be out here? I wonder, knowing the answer. Nobody.

"I am still on the trail, Mr. Midnight," Ritzi pipes up in a raspy little bark.

She is feeling the lack of water, and so am I.

We have walked at least a mile and I begin to wonder how an accomplice stuck out here can get a stolen necklace to L.A. posthaste.

Ritzi's pink tongue is hanging down to her frilly salmon-pink chest. Even I find my tongue making an undignified escape from my mouth. When did you last see a cat pant? We are in deep trouble.

Ritzi perks one adorable little floppy ear. That is another thing about dogs: sloppy, floppy ears and tongues. No restraint.

"Mr. Midnight! Someone is coming! Rescue!"

So floppy ears have pretty sharp hearing. I mount a dune of scrub and sand to confront the visitor, in case it is the crook with the overripe shoe. I hunch flat just below the ridge, ready to hit and run if need be.

Imagine my horror when I see not a pair of human shoes but four bare pale feet—equipped with fur and nails. This could be a wild cougar (a cousin of mine but hardly the kissing kind),

the wily coyote, or who-knows-what desert predator. Bad
news, but not unexpected.

Instead I confront…another blasted dog! White, about fifteen inches at the shoulder, powerful build and head, small
brain, freckles on the ears, and a big, stupid, toothy grin.

"Hi, little lady," he greets Ritzi, ignoring me as if I were
iguana guano. "What is a city slicker like you doing out here all
alone?"

Ritzi dances up the ridge like a Day-Glo welcoming commit-
tee. They do much disgusting dog greeting stuff: tail sniffing
and the like. Finally Ritzi turns to me.

"This is Bear, Mr. Midnight." Bear eyes me and I recognize
his breed, or part of it: pit bull. Oh, great. "Mr. Midnight is a
famous Las Vegas detective, Bear. He saved me from a dognap-
per. I am so eager to get back to my dear mistress, Miss Mitzi
Malone."

"We could use some water first," I point out. Where there is
a domesticated dog in the desert, there must be a human with a
hose.

"No problem." Bear's growl does his name justice. "I do not
normally associate with kittycats, but in my line of work I have
to get along with all kinds."

"What is your line of work?" I ask suspiciously. I have never
known a dog to work if he could lie around and beg for his supper.

"Stunt stuff," he says modestly. "Motion pictures."

Ritzi squeaks. "Oh, now I see! It is Big Bear, the movie star."

I groan. All I need is a celluloid hero on the case. And, by the way, why are dogs always hogging the screen? You do not see cats getting equal time on film. It is true that dogs will do anything for a tidbit while cats are more dignified. One would think the viewing public would prefer watching a choosy cat to a greedy mutt.

Ritzi is telling Big Bear all about the trail she has been following. After much mutual sand sniffing, Big Bear gives a gruff bark. "I recognize the scent underneath the lizard leaving: it is one of my cameramen."

"*My* cameramen," indeed. Fame does go to some heads.

So I follow the two dogs. (And they are a sight from behind, let me tell you. Not Mutt and Jeff but Bear and Babycakes.) When we mount a rise, spread out beyond is civilization: Jeeps and RVs and film equipment and people to make it all happen.

"There is my trainer." Big Bear points out a dark-haired lady in jeans and boots.

"And the cameraman?" I ask.

Bear jerks his massive jaws toward a cluster of technical crew. "Dude in the *Jurassic Park* T-shirt and Nike high-tops. Come on, Ritzi—and you too, Midnight—my trainer will give us water and food."

"It is *Mr.* Midnight to you," I say between my teeth, but the delinquent K9s are already trotting toward the eats, all thought of crime and punishment forgotten.

I follow to find them lapping up fresh food, water, and attention. After a mind-restoring drink, I sniff the vittles. Disgusting dog food. My stomach growls, but I have more on my mind than my appetite.

Fingering the perp was only Act One of this drama. What good is a crook without evidence of the crime? Somehow this guy planned to get that stolen diamond necklace en route to a California pawnshop in a flash. How? He is marooned here in the desert just like the rest of us.

I ask myself, how would *I* leave here if I had to get back to Las Vegas fast? Easy. I would hop a vehicle heading in that direction. Even now a Jeep is revving its engine for an errand somewhere.

I edge up to the Nike high-tops and sniff them until the dude lifts a foot to nudge me away. Yup, the sneaker tread is the same pattern we have been trailing, and I smell something that a lizard might leave on the bottom of one.

Then another smell overcomes the bad one. The strong, unmistakable scent of fresh tuna fish on whole wheat. *Yum, yum.* My tummy writhes in excitement. It has been a long, lunchless night and I have not talked turkey with my friend Charlie the Tuna in some time. The dude eyes me and kicks out again. I growl and edge away. I have got to find the diamonds before they are history.

Where? I glance back at the snarfing dogs. Show them a little food and they would forget where their own tails were! It is up to me, even if I must do it on an empty stomach.

I sniff around the various vehicles and pause finally at the idling Jeep. A guy at the wheel is tapping his fingers on the dashboard in time to a Rolling Stones tape.

"Hurry up!" he yells. "I gotta get this film back to the studio today, you know."

I hop up on the passenger seat.

"Hey, cat, where did you come from? Want to hitch a ride to Hollywood?"

See how easy it is to get from A to Z, from L.V. to L.A., even from nowhere to fame and fortune?

"Here's the film, now quit complaining," says another man. A stack of film canisters hovers over me like a big black metal king in a game of checkers. Before I can be crowned, I leap to the floorboard. Something is fishy.

I have never before been so close to movie-making magic and lean up to paw the canisters. My nose has been this close to essence of tuna fish before, though. One canister reeks with it. Naughty, naughty fishy fingers give the game away.

"Bye-bye, kitty," the driver is saying, shifting into gear. "I got to blow this place now."

And I got to solve this case now. But how…?

I claw the canisters, knocking them over. The driver curses, but I follow the tuna-fish trail, pawing and nosing until, with a wrench, the top lid flips off…

And, rattling like a crystal snake, out tumbles a length of di-amonds.

"Holy cats!" the driver shouts. "Someone stuck a prop in here instead of film."

I eye him innocently. His eyes narrow as he studies me.

"Or is it really a prop? There are no diamond necklaces in this low-budget epic. Hey, where's our security man? And where the devil did this cat come from?"

Well, I do not like long, drawn-out endings in real life any more than I do in reel life. Let us say that in due time I inherit a slightly used tuna fish sandwich.

By midafternoon—thanks to an Academy-Award performance by Big Bear, who stands by the cameraman crook and growls, ignoring all commands from his trainer—the diamonds, film canister, Ritzi, and I are on our way back to Las Vegas and the Metropolitan Police Department. The cameraman returns as well, in a separate vehicle in special custody.

By nightfall, I am restored to my red velvet pillow in the Goliath dressing room, Ritzi is installed in a new canvas carrier, and the real diamonds are returned to their chic black velvet case.

Miss Mitzi is donning the real diamonds for that night's performance, with no one but the police and the crooks the wiser. Once Ritzi was rescued—and the police recognized her as Miss Mitzi's—any tears she might have shed for the treacherous Lennie the Ferret were overtaken by tears of joy at Ritzi's return (and my own, I assume).

I watch Miss Mitzi link the seven strands of sparkling diamonds around her dainty neck. Much as I hate to admit it, these gems would not be back in their proper place if I had not had help from a couple of...dogs. I guess there is room for all kinds in this world, except crooks.

I also realize that the necklace that Miss Mitzi wears to such advantage is the kind known as a dog collar. Perhaps it is poetic justice that the thief of a dog collar should be collared by a dog. Or two.

As for me, I would not wear a collar of any kind, under any

circumstances. That is why cats are cool dudes who get to come and go without leashes and sleep on red velvet pillows, and dogs are, well, just dogs, after all is said and done.

Case closed.

In the beginning, we both thought that collaborating on a story would be far easier than it turned out to be.

We quickly agreed on the age of our protagonist—thirteen—but then we got mired in the type of mystery or suspense story we wanted to write. Wendy loves secret passageways and locked room puzzles; Alyson prefers the mysteries of the human heart.

We went over at least a dozen plot lines, rejecting every one, until Wendy asked Aly, "What is the scariest situation an eight grader can find herself in?"

Alyson answered, "Lunch period at a middle school, especially if you're new."

From that point, our story flowed.

"Be Your Own Best Friend" is a story of psychological suspense. We enjoyed writing it together. We hope you enjoy reading it.

BE YOUR OWN BEST FRIEND

BY Wendy Hornsby
AND Alyson Hornsby

Red, gooey, disgusting Sloppy Joe filling oozed out of Carey's sandwich and glopped into her lap before she could catch it with her napkin. A grimace formed on her already gloomy face. Several kids sitting near her at the lunch benches looked over and giggled. Carey raised her chin and looked at them. She tried to smile as if she weren't embarrassed while she dabbed at the spreading mess on her lap.

Carey wished that her mom hadn't given her such a messy lunch. Ever since Mom had been transferred to Findlay Creek, lunch was usually dinner leftovers—even if dinner had been takeout.

Feeling as red in the face as the stain on her jeans, Carey gathered the remains of her lunch and carried them over to the trash cans. A second, smaller red glob dropped on her clothes in the process.

As she walked past the other kids, she wished at least one of them would call her over to talk, or just say something, anything, to her. She tried to smile and make eye contact, but everyone already seemed to have forgotten she was ever there. The other eighth graders at the lunch benches just continued to chat with their own little groups, looking cozy and content.

In every new school, it was always the same for Carey. Findlay Creek Middle School was her sixth new school in the two years since her parents' divorce. Being the new kid all the time was difficult, especially for someone as shy as Carey. She tried her best to meet people. She tried to look like someone who could be a friend, but every time she finally broke through the barrier of silence and met someone she could talk with at school, Mom would be assigned to a new project at work. They would move, and Carey would have to start all over.

"You'll make new friends," Mom always said.

Carey wanted to know how you were supposed to make *new* friends when you never had old friends!

There had been a time, in Kansas, when Carey had saved herself from being devoured whole by the monster of loneliness. She had made up a friend to talk to. Talking to herself had made everyone, especially her mother, think she was nuts.

Carey wiped her hands and sat back down on the end of the bench with her knees tucked up to her chest to hide the stain on her jeans. She peered off through the fence beyond the basketball court and tried to appear fascinated with the brown grass and withering flowers on the far side. If she had to be alone, at least she wanted to appear as if she were alone on purpose. Her one consolation was that Monday was half over. Only four more lunch periods to endure that week.

That evening, Carey was in her bedroom, finishing her

homework, when her mother came home. Mrs. Parker rushed into her daughter's room. Before Carey could say anything, her mother went into a long speech about the details of her hectic day. She paused only long enough to plant a light kiss on Carey's forehead. Carey sat patiently, as she always did, waiting for Mom to finish. After at least ten minutes, the usual questions came.

"How was your day, dear?"

"Same as every day," Carey said, shrugging her shoulders.

"Meet anyone interesting?" Mrs. Parker slipped off her high heels and sat on the bed beside Carey. She combed her fingers through her daughter's curly hair as if trying to bring some order to the unruly mass. "I hope you're making an effort. I don't want a repeat of what happened in Kansas. Remember what Dr. Osgood told you, 'You have to *be* a friend to have a friend...'"

"I try, Mom. But everyone is in a group, and they don't want me around. Small towns are the worst. Everyone has been friends since kindergarten. They look at me as if I'm an alien."

"Nonsense. It's all in your attitude. I moved around a lot as a kid. It isn't so difficult if you put some effort into it."

"But you're outgoing, and I'm not. I'm too weird, Mom. Nobody wants me around."

"You're certainly silly." Mrs. Parker showed her impatience with her daughter. "Analyze the problem, then find a solution. What do you want, Carey?"

"What do I want?" Carey faced her mother squarely. "I want to go home. I want Dad and Grandma and all my friends living on our same street again, the way it used to be. I want someone to know who I am."

"Then go out and introduce yourself to someone." Mrs. Parker picked up her shoes. "Dinner in twenty minutes."

When her mother was safely out of earshot, slipping something into the microwave no doubt, Carey dared to mimic her mom quoting Dr. Osgood, the nerdy psychiatrist in Kansas: "Be your own best friend. You're only as lonely as you want to be." Dr. Osgood had spouted the same dopey clichés to her every day of the two weeks she was stuck in his clinic. "When the world hands you lemons, make lemonade."

The microwave dinged. Dinner was ready.

Tuesday morning, Carey walked to school reciting Dr. Osgood's clichés to herself. At first, she only ran them over in her mind, but pretty soon, she was saying them out loud, imitating the fat-nosed doctor. Then she started answering him back. She didn't realize how loud she was speaking until, two blocks from school, the red-headed girl Brooke, who sat in front of her during Spanish class, turned around and gave her a look as if, truly, Carey was completely nuts.

"Who are you talking to?" Brooke asked.

"Myself," Carey answered.

Brooke waited for her to catch up. "What are you talking about, then?"

"Reciting my Spanish. *Dónde esta el baño?*" Carey said, too embarrassed to tell her the truth.

"*El baño esta...*" was as far as Brooke got before she started to laugh. "I always think that means the boys' bathroom. Shouldn't the girls' bathroom be *la baña?*"

Carey felt herself blush, but for once she didn't duck her head and drop back. Instead, she laughed right along with Brooke. It felt so good to walk with someone across campus that she almost couldn't stop laughing after the bell rang. For the first time in a very long time, Carey had someone to eat lunch with.

After school, Carey rushed to find Brooke.

"La baña esta en mi casa," Brooke said, tugging Carey's backpack. "And that's where I'm going. My house, that is. Want to come? You live on the same block as me. I watched you move in. Your mom works with my dad. Actually, your mom took over my dad's old job. My dad was assigned to a new project."

"Every time my mom gets a new project," Carey said, "we move."

"Same with us. We're leaving in a week. Albuquerque, New Mexico, this time."

Carey suddenly felt like crying, and she could see that Brooke was unhappy, too. They had just met, and now Carey was going to lose her only friend.

For the next week Carey and Brooke were almost inseparable. Finally, Carey had someone who knew about her life. Really knew about her. Carey's mother and Brooke's father had been playing a sort of leapfrog with each other, moving into and out of many of the same towns according to the wishes of their employer. Carey and Brooke found that they had attended several of the same schools, had lived in the same neighborhoods, and had been chased by the same big, mangy dog in Tulsa, Oklahoma. Even if they had never lived in the same place at the same time, they'd had so many similar experiences that they began to feel as if they had known each other for a very long time.

Carey and Brooke avoided talking about Brooke's upcoming move until the afternoon of the last day. Brooke had treated them both to an ice cream cone. They were sitting atop a picnic table in the park, finishing their cones, when Brooke said, "I always hate moving."

"Then don't go." Carey felt close to tears. "Stay here with me."

"I did that once. I ran away and hid because I didn't want to move until the end of the school term."

"What happened?" Carey asked.

"My parents found me."

Carey had an idea that made her heart pound in her chest. "You could stay with me and my mom until the term is over. Ask your parents."

"And you could spend the summer with me," Brooke said, sounding as excited as Carey felt.

Carey grabbed Brooke by the hand and almost dragged her from the table. "There's no time to waste. Let's go call them."

When she came home from work at seven, Carey's mother skipped the usual retelling of her day. Instead, she put her arm around her daughter. "I know you'll miss Brooke, Carey. But imagine how much her parents would miss her if she stayed here with us. All is not lost, though. Her parents and I have decided that we'll send the two of you to the same camp this summer."

"This summer?" Carey's throat seemed to close up, choking back the words she wanted to say.

"Summer is only a few months away."

Carey knew that summer was exactly fifty-two lunch periods away.

Mom slipped out of her heels. "You've made one friend already. You can make another." Then she walked off toward the kitchen, leaving Carey to fight back her tears alone.

The next morning, moving day, dawned cold and gray. Carey thought that the weather suited the occasion perfectly. Feeling sad, she walked over to Brooke's house.

Brooke met her with a big hug. "Don't forget me, Carey."

"Don't go," Carey begged, and then felt ashamed when Brooke started to cry.

Brooke's mother came over and said it was time to leave. "Brooke will write to you as soon as we get to Albuquerque. Summer will be here sooner than you think."

Then Brooke was gone.

That night, it rained. Not a little rain, but a huge storm with thunder and lightning and water pouring down in a relentless torrent. Carey's mother called from downtown. "It's raining so hard, it isn't safe for me to drive. I'll be home as soon as I can get there. Make yourself some dinner and don't wait up for me."

Carey didn't feel like eating.

She sat beside her living room window, watching the rain.

She worried about Brooke's family driving through the storm. And she worried about going to school the next day, all alone again.

The night was so dark that the window mirrored the lighted room behind her. Carey leaned her forehead against the cold pane and looked into the reflection of her eyes on the glass, pretending they were Brooke's. "Come back," she said, and then waited for Brooke to respond.

Now and then, a gust of wind would snap a tree branch against the side of the house with a pop that sounded like someone knocking on the door. Every time it happened, Carey imagined herself opening the door and finding Brooke standing there. And then she imagined what they would say to each other.

"How was the trip to Albuquerque?" Carey would ask.

"We couldn't get through," Brooke would say. "The roads were flooded."

Brooke would be wet and shivering, and Carey would bring her inside. "Come in and get warm, tell me all about it."

Thinking about her friend, pretending to have a long conversation with her, made Carey feel better. She was glad her mother was elsewhere, because she knew what would happen if Mom came in and found her talking to someone who wasn't really there.

"What do you think, Dr. Osgood?" Carey imitated her mother's voice of concern. "The girl is talking to herself again. What shall we do with her?"

"You're only as lonely as you want to be," she answered,

mocking old Dr. Osgood by speaking so deeply that it tickled her throat. "Be your own best friend."

Rain beat steadily on the roof, sounding like a constant drumroll. The room had grown cold. Carey pushed away from the window, went over to the sofa, and curled up under a quilt her grandmother had made. She didn't realize she had fallen asleep until she heard a knock at the door. At first she was certain that it was the wind and the tree again. After the third sharp rap, she decided otherwise.

Untangling herself from the quilt, she crossed the room and opened the door.

Brooke was standing under the porch light, her drenched clothes clinging to her shivering frame. She gave a little laugh and smiled at Carey.

Carey reached out to touch her friend because she was afraid that she was still asleep and that Brooke was no more than a vision in her dreams. But Brooke's arm was wet and cold and as firm and real as Carey's own. As she drew her into the living room, Carey asked Brooke, "How was the trip to Albuquerque?"

"We couldn't get through. The roads were flooded."

Carey took Brooke's wet coat and handed her the quilt that was still warm from her nap. "Where are your parents?" Carey asked.

"They're going to a hotel. They said I can stay here, if it's okay with your mom."

There was no Mom around to ask, so of course it was all right. Carey heated them a can of soup while Brooke changed

into dry clothes—one of Carey's flannel nightgowns, the one her father had sent last Christmas. After they ate, they locked the doors, turned out the lights, and climbed under the covers of Carey's twin beds. They talked through most of the night, partly because they were waiting for Carey's mom, and partly because there was so much to talk about. Sometime before dawn, they both drifted off to sleep.

By morning, the heavy rain had dwindled to a soft drizzle. When the alarm clock rang, Carey wakened, exhausted. Without disturbing Brooke, Carey got up and dressed for school. There was no reason for Brooke to get out of her warm bed that cold morning because she was no longer registered at Findlay Creek Middle School. Carey wished she could stay home, too.

As she walked toward her mother's room, Carey started making up aches and pains and various excuses why she should be excused from school. But her mother wasn't in her room. The only signs that her mother had made it home the night before were the pair of high heels left in the middle of the kitchen floor and a note propped against the toaster.

"Sorry I had to leave before you got up this morning," the note said. "Glad everything is fine. See you tonight. Love, Mom."

Carey called her mother at the office. "I have a terrible cold," she said, talking through her nose and coughing twice. She didn't mention that Brooke was there, because then Mom would know Carey's cold was only an excuse to stay home.

Promising to call if she needed anything, Carey changed

back into her nightgown and climbed back into bed. It was nearly noon when the two girls finally decided they needed food. They made a pile of cinnamon toast and spent the day in their nightclothes, watching soap operas—which they found hysterically funny—and old movies on video.

Carey's mother called three times, and every time Carey neglected to mention Brooke. Brooke's parents never called at all. Sometime around dusk, with rain falling hard once again, Carey's mother called a fourth time.

"I hate to do this to you, honey, especially since you've been cooped up all day with that cold, but I have to work late tonight," Mom said. "I'll be home by bedtime, I promise."

Carey and Brooke went to bed early and never saw Mom. On the second day, Carey pretended to dress for school, but after Mom left for work, she stayed home again. As she did on the third day, and the fourth, until a full week of school had slipped by without Carey ever facing the silent treatment at the lunch benches. Without any question, it was the best week Carey had spent during the entire past two years. She was never once, even for a minute, lonely.

Brooke's parents never called. Every evening, when Carey's mother arrived home, Brooke was already either asleep or in Carey's room reading by herself or out visiting her former neighbors. No one ever bothered to mention to Mrs. Parker that there was a houseguest, and, except for mentioning how big Carey's appetite was all of a sudden, Mrs. Parker never noticed. Not even on the weekend.

Once, on Sunday afternoon, Mrs. Parker almost walked

right into Brooke with the laundry basket. "Put your things away" was all she said. Then she handed Brooke the basket, mistaking her for her daughter! Carey had watched the close encounter and could hardly keep from laughing right out loud until she had Brooke safely inside her room with the door closed.

"When are we going to tell Mom you're here?" Carey asked.

"When my parents call," Brooke answered.

On the second Monday, the attendance office at Carey's school called, wanting to know where she had been all the previous week. At first, she was nervous about the trouble she would certainly get into. Then Brooke told her what to say.

"I have pneumonia," Carey said. "I just got out of the hospital. I don't know when I'll be back in school."

At noon, the two girls were sprawled on the living room floor in their nightgowns, going through old photo albums, laughing over Carey's pictures of her father and grandmother and all the friends who had lived down the block. The girls were so involved with the pictures that they didn't hear Carey's mother come in.

"Carey?" Mrs. Parker was as pale as if she had seen a ghost, and that ghost was Carey. "What are you doing home?"

Carey shut the album in front of her. "Nothing."

"Your school called. They said you have been absent for six days."

Carey counted. "Only five and a half days." She turned toward Brooke for confirmation, but Brooke must have seen Mom and had managed to slip away in time.

"Who were you talking to?"

"Myself. Like Dr. Osgood said, be your own best friend." She tried to laugh as if the phrase were an old familiar joke, but the look on her mom's face froze her.

Mrs. Parker placed her hand over Carey's forehead. "I'll call a doctor."

"I'm not sick."

Mrs. Parker took a deep breath as if trying to calm herself. She looked more worried than angry, and that made Carey feel terribly guilty.

"If you're not sick," Mrs. Parker said, "then why aren't you at school?"

Avoiding telling her mom something was no different from coming straight out with a lie. So instead Carrie blurted out the truth. "I stayed home because Brooke is here. She's been here since last Sunday night."

Carey expected a flood of questions, like where is Brooke, and how did she get here, and why didn't you tell me? Instead, her mother stood absolutely still and silent for an entire minute, watching her the whole time. Mrs. Parker was so pale that Carey began to feel frightened.

"I'll get Brooke," Carey said, heading for her room. "She can tell you about it."

Brooke wasn't in the bedroom. Brooke wasn't anywhere. Carey rushed into the living room, where her mother was dialing the telephone.

"Maybe she went down to the park," Carey said. "I'll go get her."

Mrs. Parker stopped her. "I picked up the mail. There's a card for you. It was postmarked two days ago." She handed her a postcard with a desert scene on the front. Holding the telephone receiver to her ear, Mrs. Parker watched her daughter study the card.

NEW MEXICO, LAND OF ENCHANTMENT was printed across the desert scene. Carey turned the card over and began to read. "'Dear Carey, *La baña esta en mi casa* in Albuquerque now.'"

"Dr. Osgood?" Mrs. Parker said into the telephone.

"'My new house is nice, but I really miss you,'" Carey read. "'I started school Thursday. Yuck!'"

"Dr. Osgood, it's happened again. Shall I bring her to you?"

"'See you next summer. Love, Brooke.'"

My twelve-year-old son, Nate, came up with the basic idea
for this story, which comes from his own experiences with
an older friend who had a paper route. His mother, Barbara
Collins (a terrific and widely published short-story writer),
worked with Nate and me on fleshing out a synopsis.

Then Nate wrote a first draft, by himself, which he also
submitted to his sixth-grade language class. I took Nate's
rough draft and fleshed it out, referring to the synopsis,
with Nate sitting next to me, making comments, sugges-
tions, and changes.

"The Chocolate-Chip Alarm" is a true family collaboration, and we hope you enjoy it.

Max Allan Collins   *Nate Collins*

THE CHOCOLATE-CHIP ALARM

BY MAX ALLAN COLLINS
AND NATHAN COLLINS

It was just another boring Wednesday, as far as Sam James was concerned. Nothing special happened in any of his eight classes at N.M.S., Northridge's only middle school, where he was in the sixth grade.

The autumn afternoon was sunny and warm as he got onto the bus for the fifteen-minute ride home. A fight broke out between two older boys, and that girl Angela sat next to him, chattering. Nothing special. Same old boring ride home...

He sat in the living room in front of the TV, with the Twinkie and glass of milk his mom had waiting for him. He aimed the remote control at the TV.

"Come on *down!*"

CLICK.

"It's the Ani-maniacs!"

CLICK.

"...the two alleged bank robbers escaped custody early this..."

CLICK.

"...I'm hunting wabbits..."

CLICK.

"Live on tape from the..."

CLICK.

Sam turned off the TV and trudged into the kitchen with his empty milk glass and plate, grumbling.

"What's wrong?" his mother asked him.

"I'm bored," he said, scowling. "There's nothing on TV."

"Maybe you should find something better to do with your time," she said.

"Good idea, Mom," he said. He didn't sound sarcastic—he didn't want to get on the bad side of somebody who gave him Twinkies and milk, after all.

As he moved back into the living room, the phone by his dad's chair rang.

"Y'ello," Sam said. "James residence."

"Hey, it's Scott."

"Hey, Scott."

"You still interested in taking over my route?"

"*Am* I!"

Sam had been after Scott for months about taking over Scott's paper route. The job paid a hundred bucks a month!

"I'm having trouble swinging both my route *and* football practice. So I have to give up my route, or get cut from the squad."

"I'm your man."

"Great," Scott said. "I'm just getting ready to take my papers out now. This is the perfect chance for you to get the hang of things—today is the day I collect."

"Does that include that old hag on Fairview?"

"Yeah," Scott said, "but she probably won't even answer the door. She's been ducking me. Some of these old people are short on dough, you know. Fixed incomes."

"Don't tell me you feel *sorry* for her! Last time I helped you deliver, she screamed at us!"

"Well, I did miss her porch and hit her rosebush. Look, I have to get started. Can you meet me at the corner of Fourth and Cannon, in five minutes?"

"Make it four," Sam said, and—with a quick word of explanation to his mom—flew out of the house.

Soon he and Scott were delivering the papers in the quiet little neighborhood where most of the houses were small and neat. And so were their lawns.

"There's no kids on this block," Sam said. "Just old people."

"They're retired, mostly," Scott said. He was fourteen and taller than Sam.

"It's like a grandparents' convention," Sam said. "Only these geezers are not near as *nice* as grandparents..."

"A lot of them are," Scott said as he hurled a paper onto a porch with precision. "They're just a little fussy sometimes."

"Fussy!" Sam said. "Cranky is more like it! 'Put the paper in the mailbox!' 'Don't walk on the lawn!' 'Leave my dog alone!' That dog was chasing *us!*"

"Most of them aren't so bad," Scott insisted. "Don't judge all of them by that grouchy old witch on Fairview."

Sam and Scott were halfway through the route when they

came to 301 Fairview. Sam stared at the house. "I'll just wait here," he said.

"No way," Scott said. "If you're going to take over for me, you better get used to dealing with these people. I'll introduce you…"

Reluctantly, Sam accompanied Scott to the front door of the slightly run-down clapboard home with its overgrown yard. Of all the houses on this block, this was the least neat—and the one most likely to house an old witch.

Scott rang the doorbell.

There was no answer.

Scott tried again.

And again, there was no answer.

"See?" Scott said. "Told you she was ducking me. You lucked out. You don't even have to—"

The door flung open.

And there the "old witch" was standing—wearing a big smile!

"How wonderful to see you dear boys," she said.

Sam almost said, "Huh?" But there was something about the old lady's eyes that bothered him. Her mouth was smiling, but her eyes weren't. They weren't mean, either—they were *frightened*.

She was digging in her purse, getting out some money.

"Here's what I owe you. I'm sorry I can't offer you chocolate-chip cookies again, like I did yesterday."

Scott started to say something, but Sam nudged him to be quiet.

"That's okay, ma'am," Sam said. "But those cookies sure were delicious."

Now Scott was the one who looked like he might say, "Huh?" But Sam nudged him again, and Scott said, "Yeah, uh…thanks. They were real good."

"Maybe tomorrow, boys," she said, with that frozen smile, as she closed the door on them.

Scott started to say something to Sam, but Sam raised a finger to his lips, shushing his friend. The younger boy pulled the older one along by the arm, until they were down the sidewalk and around the corner.

"I don't know who's crazier," Scott said, "you or that old lady!"

"Probably me…but something's wrong in that house."

Scott rolled his eyes. "You know as well as I do that that witch never gave us any chocolate-chip cookies, not yesterday or *ever!*"

"Don't you get it?" Sam asked. "She was trying to signal us!"

"Signal us?"

"Sure! Everything she did would seem normal to anybody but us! She was friendly, paid her bill, talked about imaginary cookies…"

"You lost me."

"She was trying to sound an alarm without *somebody* in the house realizing it."

Scott really rolled his eyes this time. "*Now* I know who's crazier…it's you!"

"Well, at least let's check it out…"

"What, peek in her window?"

Now it was Sam's turn to roll his eyes. "You have a better idea?"

"Sure," Scott said, and started to walk away, lugging his heavy bag of papers. "Finish my route…"

"Well, I'm checking this out," Sam said, and headed back toward the old woman's house.

Scott sighed, then stopped. "Maybe *I'm* the craziest," he muttered, and ran to catch up with the younger boy.

The two boys quietly sneaked around the side of the house. They worked their way behind some shrubs and found a window in which the shade was not drawn all the way down. They could see under it, into the old lady's living room….

Two men were standing, talking to each other. Almost arguing, really. One was tall and skinny, the other short and chubby. Both needed shaves, wore jeans and plaid shirts, and had guns stuck in their belts.

The old lady was there, too. She was sitting in a wooden chair—tied to it. There was a gag in her mouth.

Sam pulled at Scott's sleeve, and the boys moved away from the window and out of the shrubs. They knelt behind a bush.

"Who are those guys?" Scott asked. He was shaking a little.

"I just saw 'em on TV," Sam said, "when I was channel-surfing."

"Those guys are *actors?*"

"Yeah, they're pretending they kidnapped the old lady," Sam said sarcastically. "Duh! They're those bank robbers that escaped this morning!"

"I heard about that on the radio, in the car," Scott said, thinking it through. "They're probably using the old lady's house to hide out in."

"You go call 911," Sam said, "and I'll stay here and keep an eye on things."

Scott nodded. "Don't do anything till the cops get here, okay?"

"I'm no hero," Sam said. "Go!"

Scott handed Sam his newspaper bag. "I can move faster without this."

"Fine," Sam said. "My house is closer than yours. Go use the phone there!"

Scott nodded again and ran off.

Soon Sam was behind the shrubs, at the window again, listening. Though the sound was muffled, he could make out the words.

The tall robber was saying, "I say we get out of here soon as it's dark."

The chubby one said, "Let's go now. Why wait? It's been ten hours. The cops won't be looking for us to be in town after all this time."

The tall one nodded. "You may be right." Now he seemed to be addressing the bound-and-gagged old woman. Her eyes were very frightened. "You've been a good hostess, grandma—but all good things come to an end."

The chubby one frowned, almost sadly. "Do we *have* to, Clete?"

Clete—which was the tall one's name, apparently—looked

at his chubby partner. "Now that you've used my name, we *really* have to…"

Crouched in the bushes, Sam felt a chill. He knew what they were saying: They were going to murder the old woman!

There was no time to wait. He had to do something *now*….

First, he dumped the papers from the newspaper bag into a pile beside the bushes.

Next, quietly, he went to the back of the house. There was a back porch with four cement steps leading to a wooden landing and a back door. He went up the steps. The wood of the landing was old, almost rotting. It creaked under Sam's footsteps.

Then Sam began to stomp his feet, trampling around as loud as he could, making as much noise as possible.

"What was that?" came Clete's shout from within the house.

Sam plastered his back against the side of the house, next to the back door, out of sight. His fingers held on to the leather strap of the empty newspaper bag.

When Clete came rushing out, Sam reached up and snagged the tall man's head and shoulders with the empty bag, pulling it down over him.

Sam yanked the bag closed and worked the strap into a knot, snugging the knot tight and shoving the robber off the porch. The robber was kicking and swearing, till he fell with a *whump*, his head hitting on one of the cement steps.

This silenced him.

The other robber—the chubby one—came out the door, too, looking confused and worried.

When the robber saw Sam—holding in two hands the gun he'd taken from the other thief's belt—the chubby man's confusion cleared up. But he still looked pretty worried as he raised his hands in the air, his own gun still tucked in his belt.

A police siren wailed in the otherwise quiet afternoon, announcing help on the way.

Before long, both the police and Scott arrived. Several officers carted the two thieves off to a squad car. The old woman was crying in relief as another officer untied her. They walked her outside and took her to an ambulance.

"Was she hurt?" Sam asked a policeman.

"No," the officer said. "But she's been through a lot. It's just a precaution."

That was a relief to Sam, who turned to Scott. The two boys grinned at each other and shared a high-five.

"Is this an exciting job I'm giving up to you," Scott asked, "or *what?*"

The next afternoon, two unusual events made yet another boring Thursday a little bit special.

First, the papers Sam was delivering had an interesting headline: PAPERBOY CAPTURES ROBBERS. It was pretty cool, even if they did spell his middle name wrong.

Second, the old lady—who was back at home already, and whose name was Mrs. Pierce—really did have a plate of chocolate-chip cookies waiting for him this time.

And she was smiling, too, with her mouth *and* her eyes.

The cookies tasted great. Too bad Scott didn't get any—Sam hoped his friend was enjoying football practice.

As for Sam, he was happy to have an after-school job.

And in the weeks that followed, life seemed a lot less boring to Sam. His paper-route customers didn't all have plates of cookies for him.

But most of them had smiles.

Laura, who is six years old, came up with the idea for the story by listening to her big sister's boyfriend talking about his job at a nursing home.

Spencer, age seven, figured out how to find out what the man would be typing by putting paper into the typewriter, and Laura decided that the mystery would be that the man's sister had been missing since she was a little girl. Spencer worked out what happened to the little girl and how to go about finding her after all these years.

Sharyn McCrumb, Spencer and Laura's mom, did most of the wording. She would read drafts of it to Spencer and Laura, and they would suggest changes and make sure that not too many big words were used. Finally, they came up with a story that everyone was happy with. Laura is especially pleased with the ending.

Sharyn McCrumb

Layla McCromb

Spencer mccrumb

TYPEWRITER MAN

BY SHARYN McCRUMB,
SPENCER McCRUMB, AND LAURA McCRUMB

Working at Northfield Nursing Home isn't nearly as boring as you think, even if it is a building full of old people. It's not as if I'm a volunteer or anything, all right? I mean, they pay me. Less than I'm worth, I admit, but it's enough to keep me in video games and halfway decent sneakers.

Ever since my dad died of cancer last year, money has been a little tight at home. My mom went back to work full-time. She's a registered nurse, and now she works as the nursing supervisor at Northfield. When she told me that the home was short on orderlies and suggested that they could use a responsible twelve-year-old for a few hours a week, I jumped at the chance.

I work part-time, late afternoons and weekends, with time off during soccer season. (We almost made it to the play-offs last year.) It makes me feel good to know that I'm helping out with expenses, even if they are mostly *my* expenses.

Working at Northfield isn't exactly taxing labor. I load the dishwashers, and I go down to the basement laundry, where I gather up the clean sheets and towels, then deliver them to the four residential floors for the housekeeping staff.

Everybody told me that there is a ghost in the basement, because the morgue is right next to the laundry. I always turn all the lights on when I go down there, and I don't waste any time. Frankly, I've never seen anything weird, even though Kenny Jeffreys swears he once saw the top half of a guy in a Confederate uniform. Just the *top half.* Too strange for me, man. The live ones around here are bizarre enough.

I see them every evening when I push the meal trolley around the halls, delivering dinner. It doesn't take me long to scope out the residents: there are senile ones, who barely notice me; feeble but chatty ones who treat me like a grandson, which is nice; and then there are a few space cadets.

Mrs. Graham in room 239 always has to have *two* dinner trays taken to her. One for her and one for her husband, Lincoln. That's her *late* husband, Lincoln, you understand. Mr. Graham left the planet in '85, but he still gets a dinner tray. And, no, he doesn't eat it. I go back at seven to pick up the trays, and his is never touched.

Mrs. Whitbread in 202 has an evil twin. Yeah, in the mirror. She's always scolding the mirror twin, telling her what a hag she is and how she ought to behave herself. I swear I'm not making this up. You can ask Kenny Jeffreys, the orderly who works the same hours I do.

Kenny's in his second year at the community college, majoring in health care. He's working for tuition and car insurance money, plus of course the experience in health care, which does not seem to excite him too much. He talks about changing his career goal to TV anchorman, but as far as I know, he's still in health care.

Northfield has its share of oddities, from ghosts to dotty old folks, but the patient who really got to me was the white-haired guy in 226. He was weirder than all the others put together. Kenny calls him "Typewriter Man."

The name on his door is Mr. Pierce, and you never see him out of his room, or wearing anything except a robe and pajamas. Every time I go into his room with the meal tray, Mr. Pierce is sitting in front of his old non-electric typewriter, tapping away like mad. He must be doing fifty words a minute. Never stops. Never looks up when you set his food down. Just keeps typing, as if it's some urgent report he's got to finish.

Only there's no paper in the typewriter. Ever.

And he just keeps typing away.

"What do you think Mr. Pierce is writing that's so important?" I asked Kenny one evening when I had delivered the supper tray through another burst of paperless typing in 226.

Kenny shrugged. "Beats me," he said. "Why don't you ask him?"

"He never looks up. He never stops typing or even notices that I'm there."

"Guess you'll never know then, kid," said Kenny, wheeling the laundry cart toward the elevator.

But I wasn't willing to give up. And I came up with an idea that might work.

The next afternoon when I showed up for work, I dropped by my mom's office and took about twenty sheets of typing paper from the bottom drawer of her desk. She wasn't there at the time, and I knew she'd never miss it. Then I went upstairs to room 226 and tapped on the door before I let myself in.

Mr. Pierce was asleep in front of his television, snoring gently. This didn't surprise me. After all, not even weird people can type twenty-four hours a day. I tiptoed up to his desk and stuck a sheet of paper in the empty typewriter. "Pleasant dreams, Mr. Pierce," I whispered as I crept away. "I'll be back to check on you at mealtime."

Two hours later, I was pushing the dinner trolley from room to room, tingling with excitement. I told the grandmotherly types about my history project. I asked Mrs. Graham how her invisible husband was doing. But the entire time my mind was on Mr. Pierce and his typewriter.

Finally, I reached room 226 and heard the familiar tapping sounds through the door. I knocked once and let myself in, calling out, "Suppertime, Mr. Pierce!" just as I always did, despite the fact that Mr. Pierce never, ever answered back.

I set the tray on the empty desk space beside the typewriter, moving as slowly as I could so that I could see what he was typing. The paper was still in place, and it was covered with words. I didn't have to take the paper, because I could memorize the whole thing in ten seconds. It was the same sentence over and over: *Alva, please come back. I'm sorry. Please come back.*

I looked at Mr. Pierce, but he was hunched over his plate, shoveling in food and ignoring me, the way he always did. I wished him a good evening and went to find Kenny.

"He just keeps typing the same sentence," I told him. "He's

telling someone named Alva to please come back, and he says he's sorry."

"Maybe it's his wife," said Kenny. "I wonder if she knows where he is."

"Somebody had to sign him in here," I pointed out.

"Maybe it wasn't her, though. Maybe they got divorced, and his kids put him here. Maybe she misses him now. A list of his relatives would probably be entered in his records folder." Kenny reads a lot of paperback mysteries while he's doing the laundry in the basement. He says it keeps his mind off the ghosts. He looked at me slyly. "Of course, I couldn't look in those folders, but since they're in your mom's office..."

"I'll see what I can do," I muttered. I felt sorry for Mr. Pierce, typing that same sad sentence day after day with no hope of getting an answer. Maybe there *was* hope, though.

The next evening I pushed my meal cart up close to Kenny's trolley full of towels. "So much for your theories, Sherlock," I told him. "I read Mr. Pierce's folder while Mom was at the photocopy machine. She almost caught me, too! Anyhow, his wife's name was Rosalie, and she died the year he was admitted to Northfield. They didn't have any children, which is probably why he's here. There was no mention of anyone named Alva in his folder."

"Has he always lived around here?" Kenny asked.

"I think so. Why?"

"You could ask one of the local old ladies if she knew Mr. Pierce before he came here to the home, and if there was ever anyone named Alva in his life. It's not a very common name. Sounds old-fashioned to me."

I couldn't think of any better ideas, and Mr. Pierce certainly wasn't talking. So the next evening when I delivered the meals, I talked with all the residents who weren't gaga. I asked if they'd always lived around here, and then asked about Mr. Pierce. It was Mrs. Graham who knew him from the old days.

"Francis Pierce!" she said, smiling. "Yes, we've known him forever, haven't we, dear?" That last remark was addressed to the invisible (deceased) Mr. Graham, and I am happy to say that he did not reply.

"Well, do you know of anyone called Alva that he once knew?"

"Alva Pierce. I hadn't thought about her in years. It was front-page news at the time, though."

She knew! I almost dropped the tray, which wouldn't have mattered, because it was Mr. Graham's and he still hadn't come back from the hereafter for spaghetti and Jell-O. But still it would have been a mess to clean up, and suddenly I felt I needed every minute of extra time I could manage.

"Was Alva his wife, then?" I asked, trying to sound polite and casual about it.

"No, dear, his sister. Such a sad thing. People did wonder if it was murder—" She looked up at me then (or maybe Mr. Graham tipped her off). She seemed to realize that she was about to talk scandal to a twelve-year-old kid. Smiling at me, she said, "Well, never mind, dear. It was a long time ago, and I expect you have a good many meals to deliver."

I could see that I wasn't going to be able to talk her into finishing the story, so I went back to delivering dinners. But my mind was going ninety miles an hour, trying to figure out another way to find out about Alva.

"You seem preoccupied tonight, young man." It was Mr. Lagerveld, who was a really nice guy, even if he didn't care too much for the food. I could tell he was in no hurry to get to his spaghetti. He had been a college professor years ago, and I liked to talk to him anyhow. I was thinking: *If I can just word the question right, maybe Mr. L. can help me.*

"I have to do some research," I told him as I set his tray down on the table and rustled up his silverware. "It's for school. It's about something that happened around here about sixty years ago, and I don't know how to go about finding the information."

"Sixty years ago? The Great Depression?"

I shook my head. "A local thing—like a person got kidnapped or something." I was guessing about the time and the event, but I thought I had the general idea anyhow.

"Have you tried looking in the newspapers?"

"How would I find a sixty-year-old newspaper? They'd fall apart, wouldn't they?"

He sighed. "No wonder my students couldn't do research. What do they teach you these days? How to find your hamster?"

"We use encyclopedias to look up stuff, but there wouldn't be anything local in the *Britannica.*"

"That is correct. So you need newspapers. Go to a library,

and ask the nice librarian for the microfilm. You see, they put old newspapers on microfilm, so they won't fall apart when grubby-handed kids use them to do history reports." He sounded gruff, but he was grinning at me, and I think he suspected that what I wanted to find wasn't an assignment for school.

"Microfilm. The public library will have papers from sixty years ago?"

"I hope so. Our tax dollars at work, young man. Good luck with your investigation. And if you ever have a question about geology—*that* I can help with."

I had to wait until Sunday afternoon to see if Mr. Lagerveld was right about the microfilm. Because I didn't have a date to go by, I knew I was going to have to scroll through about ten years' worth of newspapers to see what happened to Alva. I just hoped Mrs. Graham was right about the story being front-page news.

Mom was delighted to take me to the library for a change, instead of to the video store, which is my usual Sunday afternoon destination. I told her I'd be a couple of hours getting material for my report. She gave me a dollar's worth of change for the photocopy machine and went off to the grocery store, happy in the knowledge that her kid had suddenly become so studious. I hated to disappoint her. I'd try to score a few A's on the old report card to bolster her faith in the new me. Meanwhile, I had to find someone named Alva.

Earlier in the week, I had figured out a way to narrow down

the newspaper search to the smallest possible number of years. I looked up Mr. Pierce's age in his record file. He was seventy-six. That meant that he was born in 1920. But Mrs. Graham remembered the case, and she was only seventy-two. I figured that she had to have been at least seven years old to remember a local tragedy—which meant that 1931 was the first year I planned to search. Mr. Pierce would have been eleven years old. I didn't know if Alva was his younger sister or an older one.

The librarian was very helpful. She showed me how to use the microfilm machines, and she showed me where the reels were kept, all carefully labeled by month and year. I started with January 1931, and flipped through day by day, reading the headlines of each front-page story. An hour and a half later I was in June of 1932, and there it was: LOCAL GIRL MISSING: BELIEVED LOST IN WOODS.

There was a drawing of a pretty girl who looked about eight years old. The story said that Alva Pierce had followed her big brother Francis into the woods, where he was playing with two other boys. They ran off and left the little girl, telling her to go back home. When they came out of the woods at suppertime, they discovered that little Alva had not returned home. The boys, their parents, and the whole neighborhood searched the woods, calling for the little girl, but she was not to be found.

I kept checking the newspapers, day after day, to see what happened to Alva Pierce. One day they brought in dogs. Another day they questioned everybody who had used the nearby road. After a week, the stories got smaller and smaller, and they were no longer on the front page. Finally the stories stopped altogether.

Alva Pierce had never been found.

"Well, now you know," said Kenny Jeffreys when I showed him the articles I photocopied from the microfilm newspapers. "Mr. Pierce was responsible for his sister getting lost in the woods, and he still feels guilty about it after all these years."

"It's because they never found her," I said. "I'll bet he still wonders what happened to her."

"Poor old guy," said Kenny, loading the last of the towels on his trolley. "Well, gotta go now. Too bad we can't help Mr. Pierce."

"I'm not ready to give up," I said. "I looked up the patch of woods that Alva got lost in back in 1932."

"Dream on, kid," said Kenny. "If no one has found that little girl after sixty-something years, I don't think your chances are all that good."

"I'm not giving up yet. I got a topographical map of the woods—the librarian suggested it. And I have one more person who might be able to help."

That evening I took Mr. Lagerveld his Salisbury steak. Before he could ask if it was Roy Rogers's horse, the way he always did, I said, "Remember how you said I could come to you if I ever had a geology question?"

"I don't do term papers," he warned me.

I pulled out my newspaper articles and my photocopied

map of the woods. "Look at this, Mr. L. This was my library project. A little girl got lost in these woods sixty years ago, and they never found her. If you were going to look for her, where would you start?"

He put on his reading glasses and studied the map and the fine print at the bottom that told where it was, and he muttered to himself some. Finally, he said, "Strictly speaking, this is geography, but I think I can help you out. People looked a couple of days in these woods and didn't find her?"

I nodded.

"Did they try the caves?"

"What caves?" I looked at the article. I didn't remember anything about caves.

"Look at this analysis of the land. Limestone. Creek nearby. Of course there are caves. But the opening might be too small for an adult to notice. Low to the ground, maybe. A little girl would find it easily enough." He took off his glasses and glared at me. "Please note that I am not advising you to go caving alone. Remember what happened to that little girl."

"No problem," I said. "I know just the person to take with me."

Saturday morning was sort of cold and drizzly, and Kenny was full of complaints, because he hated to get up early on Saturday, and he was missing a trip to the movies with his friends, and there were about a dozen other gripes. But he had agreed that I ought not to go alone, and he was curious about the little girl's disappearance, so, with a lot of grumbling, he picked me up at my house at seven A.M. and told my mother we were going hiking, which was partly true.

The house that had belonged to the Pierce family was in ruins now, but it was still there, so we parked the car nearby. Then we set off on foot from its backyard. That's the way Mr. Pierce and Alva would have gone. We had knapsacks with food, rope, and flashlights, and Kenny had brought a shovel in case we needed it, but he said we had to take turns carrying it.

The woods hadn't changed much in sixty years. It was still a rural part of the county, thick with underbrush and easy to get lost in. I stayed close to Kenny and tried not to think about snakes.

We followed the creek, examining boulders, ridges, and any kind of land formation that might hide an opening to a cave. Because it was early March, I thought we might have a better chance of finding a cave than the searchers would have had in June, when summer plants had covered everything with vines and grasses. We walked around for hours, getting our boots muddy and snagging our trousers on brambles and old bits of barbed wire.

Finally, I sat down to rest near the stream, wishing I'd packed two more sandwiches in my knapsack. As I leaned back, putting one arm behind me for balance, I slipped and fell flat on my back. My arm had sunk into the ground.

"Kenny! Bring the shovel!" I yelled. "I think I found it!"

After all these years, mud had filled most of the entrance, but Kenny and I took turns digging like mad, and soon we had an opening big enough for me to fit into.

"I don't like the idea of you going in alone," he told me.

"At least you know where I am," I said. "If I get in trouble, you can go for help."

I tied the rope around my waist, took the flashlight, and wriggled through the muddy opening and into the darkness. "It's okay!" I yelled back to Kenny.

The cave was too low to stand up in. I stayed stooped over and inched my way along, keeping the beam of the flashlight trained at my feet so that I wouldn't tumble into a pit. I hadn't gone more than about ten feet before the light showed a flash of white on the ground in front of me. I crept forward, shivering as a trickle of water ran down the neck of my shirt, and I reached out my hand and touched—a bone.

I dug a little in the soft mud and found more bones and a few scraps of cloth. There was a large boulder near the bones, and I think it must have fallen, either killing the person or pinning her down so that she could not escape.

This was Alva. She had found the cave and had been trapped there, without anyone knowing where to look for her.

I made my way back out as quickly as I could. I hadn't thought about cave-ins until I saw the boulder beside those tiny white bones. "She's in there," I told Kenny as I gasped for fresh air. "Now we have to tell the police, I guess."

A couple of days later, I was back at work, and Mom had finished yelling at me for being a daredevil. As I took the meal tray in to room 226, I saw that Mr. Pierce was asleep, so I stopped at the desk and set a newspaper down on top of the empty typewriter. The front-page story was about Alva Pierce being found after all these years.

The search and rescue team had recovered the body, and she was buried now in the little church cemetery, next to her parents. I hoped Mr. Pierce would be glad to know that his sister had been found.

I wasn't sure, though, until I got to Mrs. Graham's room to deliver her two dinners. She took her dinner and set the other one down in front of her late husband's empty chair. Then she said, "Young man, I thought children were not allowed in Northfield except at visiting hours."

"Yes, ma'am," I said. "But I work here, remember?"

"Not you!" she snapped. "Mr. Graham tells me that he distinctly saw a little blond girl going into room 226 just now. Didn't you, dear?"

Whatever he said, I didn't hear it.

When my son Joe was a junior in high school, he started bringing me a good supply of "Joe Gorman Stories."

The stories bore the influence of both Ray Bradbury and Richard Matheson, two writers I also imitated when I was Joe's age. (And to this day, actually. A few months ago I was having some problems with story flow, and I sat down and read a Matheson that had confronted some of the same stage-management problems—and my dilemma was solved. I just "borrowed" a few tricks from Matheson.)

Joe went on to get a degree in journalism, to work as a park ranger, and to become an outdoorsman who could convert his love for nature into articles for national magazines.

I hope that he goes back to writing fiction someday. As those early stories showed, he's certainly got the talent for it.

We had a good time working with old Owlie in this particular tale, and hope that you have a good time reading about him.

THE NEW, IMPROVED OWLIE MADISON

BY ED GORMAN

AND JOE GORMAN

Once upon a time there were three bullies whose names were—

Nah. That isn't the way I want to start this.

Because if I start it "Once upon a time," you'll think I'm making it up, like a story for little kids or something. And if I start it "Once upon a time," then the first thing I've got to talk about is that night I was walking home from the library—

And that isn't what I want this story to be about.

I want this story to be about how the fourth-cutest girl in tenth grade fell in love with me...

Now right up front I've got to admit that I'm not the best-looking boy at Hoover High. I've been going to fat camp since I was in sixth grade. My eyeglasses don't help, either. I tried wearing contacts but they gave me an infection. So I wear these big, round glasses...and the kids call me "Owlie." I really hate that, but when the whole school of 1,400 kids decides to call you that, there isn't much you can do about it, is there? I guess that's why I used to stay around the house so much, you know, up in my room reading detective novels, Christopher Pike, R. L. Stine, all the great ones...

I'm telling you all this so you'll realize how surprised everybody was the sunny April morning I pulled up in the school parking lot in a shiny red convertible with Stacy Reeves, the fourth-cutest girl in tenth grade, all snuggled up to me real nice and close. To be perfectly honest, even though I was in eleventh grade and a year older, I felt a lot younger and less experienced than Stacy. Poise, I guess you'd call it. She had a lot, and I didn't have any.

You should have seen all those kids gawking at me. I wanted to laugh at them. To them, Owlie was just this dweeb who would come and go at Hoover without making any favorable impression on anybody.

Well, this was the new, improved Owlie, and they'd better get used to it.

That morning, there was an assembly in the gym, and Mr. Peterson gave his usual long, boring speech about school spirit, and how there shouldn't be any more racing in the school parking lot, and how the police were still looking for the kids who trashed three rooms on the second floor last week, and would the graffiti artists please learn to correctly *spell* the dirty words they were spraying on the walls, and how we should all give a great big Hoover welcome to today's guest, Mr. Al Culligan, who was going to show us some slides about our town at the turn of the century.

Not that I paid much attention, you understand.

I mostly concentrated on Stacy, who sat very close to me on the bleacher seat.

"I just can't wait for tonight," she whispered. "It'll be great riding around with the top down. All that wind in my hair."

"Your *beautiful* hair," I whispered back.

Then she kind of gave me a little hug.

And I quick-like looked around to see who was watching us. I wanted witnesses.

Stacy Reeves, the fourth-cutest girl in tenth grade, was giving everybody the impression that she was my girlfriend.

The day kept going pretty much like that.

We ate lunch together in the cafeteria, sat across from each other in study hall, and then managed to work on the same poor dead smelly frog in bio.

That's where we were, just leaving bio, when Mick McKulsky nailed me.

Mick McKulsky is the kind of football player who gives all athletes a bad name—big, mean, stupid, and arrogant. He's famous for trying to run cats over when he sees them in the street. He went up over a curb to get a kitty once. He missed the cat and slammed into a tree. But, being Mick McKulsky, the cops didn't give him a ticket.

Mick has two major goals in life: to get out of eleventh grade (he's been in it two years now) and to torment me every day, in every way possible.

He grabbed me and slammed me into the lockers. My books went flying and my owlie glasses slid off my nose and landed on the floor.

Now, you have to understand: for Mick, this is a slow day. On a fast day, he'll throw me down stairs, or lock me up in the janitor's closet, or de-pants me in the boys' room and then throw my pants out the window.

So getting slammed into the lockers isn't really too bad— unless you just happen to have the fourth-cutest girl in tenth grade walking beside you.

Then getting thrown into the lockers is really humiliating.

"Leave him alone!" Stacy said to Mick.

Which, actually, made this stuff even more embarrassing. Sort of like having your older sister save you from getting beaten up.

Not that Mick paid any attention, you understand.

He jerked open a locker, grabbed me by the seat of the pants—I couldn't see what he was doing, my glasses being somewhere on the floor—and started to stuff me inside the way he usually does.

By now, a lot of kids were standing around laughing—for some reason, people love it when I get picked on—but then they stopped laughing all of a sudden and a voice even meaner than Mick's said:

"Leave him alone, McKulsky, or I'll punch your ugly face in."

Mick McKulsky was still holding me a good three inches off the floor by the seat of my pants, but he was no longer trying to fit me inside the narrow locker.

"What's this all about, Crusher?" Mick asked.

"It's about him bein' a friend of ours."

"*Him?* Owlie?"

"That's what I said, ain't it? Now put him down."

"God, Crusher, if I'da known—"

He set me down.

With as much dignity as possible, which is to say not much at all, I straightened my clothes and turned around to see Crusher McGraw, Matt "Torquemada" Stivers, and Bob "Attila" Lambert standing there, glowering at Mick.

There's something I should tell you right here about the bullies at Hoover High. Not all of them are jocks, by any means. A lot of jocks are bright, decent boys and girls.

And one more thing: there are the *popular* bullies—popular because they come up with really inventive ways of persecuting dweebs like me, thereby endearing themselves to the unwashed masses who clog the halls. And then there are the *unpopular* bullies who can't ever think of anything neat to do with us dweebs and nerds. Even bullies have to have a certain sense of style.

Crusher, Torquemada, and Attila were (a) a lot bigger than Mick and (b) first-string football players. Mick was second-string.

So when they gave him an order...he obeyed.

"Jeez, Owlie," Mick said, "I'm really sorry. I didn't have no idea you was so tight with these three dudes."

Mick talks like that. He actually does.

"That's all right, Mick," I said. "But next time—"

He held up ham-sized hands in front of his face, as if I were going to punch him. "There ain't gonna be no next time, believe me," Mick said.

He wasn't looking at me. He was looking at his three betters on the football team.

"There better not be," said Atilla.

They nodded to me and left.

"You know this afternoon after bio?"

"Uh-huh."

"When Mick came up and tried to stuff you in the locker?"

"Uh-huh."

"And then those three guys came up and threatened to beat him up?"

"Uh-huh."

"Don't those boys usually beat you up themselves?"

"Uh-huh."

"Then how come they didn't?"

We were on our way home from school, top down, radio up, Stacy all snuggled tight against me.

Every time we'd stop at a light, people would look over the car and then look over Stacy and then look over me and—

Well, they were kind of surprised to see me with a car like this and a girl like that.

But I wasn't surprised.

After all, this was the new, improved Owlie.

"I guess they just decided they liked me."

"Gee, that really seems weird."

"What does?"

"You know," she said, "kids like Crusher and Torquemada and Attila just suddenly starting to like you."

I smiled over at her. "Well, *you* just suddenly started liking me."

She blushed. Just like bullies, there are degrees of popular kids. The three cutest girls in tenth grade have a lot of boys following them around all the time. The three cutest girls wouldn't have anything to do with me, even with my shiny red convertible. But the fourth-cutest girl...well, there's kind of a drop between third and fourth place. And the fourth-place girl doesn't have all that many guys chasing after her, so...

"Yeah, I guess I did, didn't I?" she said. "Just suddenly started liking you, I mean."

I patted her hand as we sped along a nice sunny stretch of road.

"It's all right."

"What's all right?" she said.

"The reason you like me."

"The reason I—"

"It's the car. Nice red convertible, who wouldn't start liking me?"

"But, Owlie, I really do—"

"A little bit you do. Like me, I mean. But you like the car a lot more."

She decided to be honest. "You're starting to grow on me. You really are, Owlie. I don't find you nearly as obnoxious as I used to."

"Does that mean we're still going to see that movie out at the mall tonight?"

"It sure does!"

☠ ☠ ☠

I dropped Stacy off just before five o'clock, then drove over to Bill's Garage.

I'd been hearing a pinging noise in the engine sometimes and I wondered if I was using the wrong kind of gas.

Bill's is where my dad and mom take their cars, too, so Bill has known me for a long time.

He told me to pull the car off the drive, over by one of the garage doors, and then he got down on his hands and knees and listened while I revved the engine.

A couple of minutes later, he stood up, wiping his hands on a rag he took from the back pocket of his garage uniform, and said, "Yeah, why don't we try some premium unleaded next time."

"Great idea," I said.

He studied the car with a look of real nostalgia on his face. "I still wish I hadn't had to sell this baby. But with two boys in college, I just couldn't afford a fancy convertible for a second car." He pointed to an old junker Ford off the drive. "That's what I'm driving these days. My wife gets the good car."

Then the phone started ringing inside the station and he had to go.

"The one thing I'll never understand, though, is why Crusher and those other two came in this morning and bought it from me—and then *gave* it to you." He shook his head, perplexed. "They sure must like you a lot, Owlie. That's a real act of generosity."

Then he was off, heading for the ringing phone.

I had an hour to go before Mom would have supper ready, so I just drove around some more. I felt as if I never wanted to leave the car. I thought about Stacy a lot, too. I really liked her.

I even managed a few kind thoughts about Crusher, Torquemada, and Attila, too.

Sure they used to beat me up every day—and make me get down on my hands and knees and bark like a dog—and throw my notebook out the window...but now we were friends.

Staying in my room and reading all those detective novels finally paid off.

You remember how Mr. Peterson said the cops were still looking for the kids who trashed three rooms on the second floor last week?

Well, it just so happened that I was walking home from the library last week when I noticed Crusher, Torquemada, and Attila running from the school.

They've been in a lot of trouble the past couple of years. If the police knew they did it, they'd get kicked out of Hoover and probably end up in reform school.

So I made them a nice little offer.

I wanted them not only to stop picking on me, I wanted them to *protect* me from all the other bullies. And I wanted that convertible of Bill's that Attila had had his eye on.

They didn't have much of a choice.

Either they went along or—

Well, that's one thing you learn from reading detective stories—how to be a real good blackmailer.

Oh...but excuse me.

I've got to go home and have some supper and then get cleaned up.

I've got a date tonight with Stacy, the fourth-cutest girl in tenth grade.

She doesn't find me nearly as obnoxious as she used to.

She really doesn't.

"The Secret Enchanted Dress" is a story that Eve started one night when she slept over at the home of her grandmother, Rita Turow. She decided she wanted to finish it so it could be in this book. Sometimes Eve made up the story and the things that people say in it, and every now and then Scott did, too. They only wrote something down if they both thought it was right.

Eve
Turow.

THE SECRET ENCHANTED DRESS

BY SCOTT TUROW
AND EVE TUROW

Once upon a time there was a little girl whose name was Jackie. She lived in a big house with her father. Her mother was gone. She did not know where.

Up in the attic, there was a box which was full of her mother's things. Often, when she was alone, Jackie would go there to look in the box. There were petticoats and sweaters, dresses and scarves. They all had a certain smell. Jackie did not know if the smell made her remember her mother, or if she only thought that was the case now.

One day her father found her in the attic.

"Those things are not yours," he said, when he saw she had opened the box. "Those things are not toys."

"I know," said Jackie. "I just wanted to look at them."

"Well, now you've seen them," her father said. "Come downstairs." Later, he said, "I'd rather you not disturb those things in the future."

"I wanted to know what they are," she said.

"They are part of the past," her father said.

After that, Jackie was careful to go to the attic only when she was sure her father was not home. The housekeeper, Mrs. Farquahrson, was somewhat chubby and could not climb the stairs to the attic.

"What are you doing?" Mrs. Farquahrson would call up the stairs.

"I am practicing ballet," Jackie answered. "One, two, three," she called, "one, two, three."

But Jackie was not practicing ballet. She was doing what she had always done. She was touching the pretty things that she had found in the box in the attic.

One day, in the box Jackie noticed a beautiful dress she had not seen before. The dress was white, with ruffles of silk and a long pink ribbon about the waist, and a small bustle that looked like a white rose. The dress, she knew, was precious. "Oh, I would love to wear that dress," Jackie thought, but she did not have the courage to touch it even with a single finger.

"What are you doing up there?" Mrs. Farquahrson called, as she often did. Jackie rushed back down the stairs.

The next day, Jackie went to the attic again. The beautiful white dress with the long pink ribbon was still in the box. Jackie stroked the dress timidly. Then she smelled the dress. Then she laid it out on a chair in the attic to admire it. After some time, she decided to put it on. It had small pink buttons along the back and she opened them carefully. Then she stepped into the dress and raised it to her shoulders.

She went to see herself in the old stand-up mirror near the light switch. But when she glanced up, she saw she was not in the attic any longer. She was in a beautiful, perfect garden. There were tall hedges around her, all trimmed evenly along the top, and neat beds thick with flowers. There were roses, peach colored and red ones, and simple buttercups. Peonies. Daisies. Dahlias. And a wide, smooth lawn.

Just at that moment, a herald sounded and she left the enclosure of the hedges. Beyond, at a distance, a parade was passing. The people in the parade were in two lines. There were men and women and they were dressed like servants, with starched shirts and aprons. Some were carrying boxes, like the box the dress had been in, while others held up dresses and suits for display. None of the clothes were as pretty as the dress Jackie was in. At the end of the line was a lonely prince, looking down sadly. He glanced her way, but Jackie ran away.

When she got back behind the hedge, she slipped out of the dress and was again in her attic. She heard Mrs. Farquahrson calling her name.

"Yes?" Jackie answered.

"My word, where have you been? I've been calling you for twenty minutes."

"I must have fallen asleep."

"Well, come down right this minute."

Jackie did.

"Oh, lands," said Mrs. Farquahrson. "There's mud all over your shoes. How did that happen?"

Jackie shrugged and said she must have stepped in a puddle when she was walking home from school. Mrs. Farquahrson seemed puzzled.

That night at dinner, her father said to her, "Mrs. Farquahrson says you've been playing in the attic."

Jackie did not answer.

"Have you been looking at those things again?" her father asked.

Jackie swore she hadn't been.

"I'm leaving a note for Mrs. Farquahrson. No more play time in the attic." Her father looked at her directly from beneath his heavy brows.

That night, when her father was asleep, Jackie went up to the attic and put on the dress. It was night in the garden, but the moon and the stars were bright. Jackie was only a little scared, but still very tired. She slept in the garden, beneath a lovely copper beech tree. In the morning when she woke, the prince stood over her. He wore a velvet doublet of blue and yellow stripes and a soft hat with a feather on the side. She was surprised to see him.

"I thought you'd *never* wake up," he said. "But then, I thought you'd never come back. Did you come to see me?"

"Sort of," Jackie said.

"My name is Frontrigo."

Jackie tried hard not to laugh. "My name is Jackie," she said.

When he heard her name, the prince covered his face with his small hand. "Your name is so amusing," he said.

"*My* name?"

They agreed to call each other F and J. They liked it better. F and J played with each other all day. As the sun began to set

on the garden, Jackie told Frontrigo, "I have to go home. My father will miss me."

"Stay," Frontrigo said. "I'm so lonely." He said he would marry her when he was old enough. He told her he was almost thirteen, but Jackie knew he was only eleven. "Please," begged Frontrigo. "You can't just come and go from a place like this."

Jackie promised that when she came back, she would stay. For now, she said, she had to go home.

She was sure her father would be angry. But instead he was sad. He covered her face with kisses and held both of her hands when he saw her come into the parlor, where he was sitting with Mrs. Farquahrson.

"I worried all day," he said. "I didn't go to work. Mrs. Farquahrson and I stayed together, hoping to find out where you had gone. Where were you?"

Jackie didn't answer.

"You ran away because of the attic, didn't you?" her father asked. "If only you could understand," he said.

Jackie ran off to her room.

The next day, when Jackie got home from school, Mrs. Farquahrson reminded her that she was not permitted to go to the attic.

"I have to go up," said Jackie. "I left something there." She was thinking of Frontrigo. She had been thinking of him all day. But Mrs. Farquahrson blocked the narrow stairway.

Jackie was still quarreling with Mrs. Farquahrson when her father came through the door from work.

"What's all this about?" he asked.

Mrs. Farquahrson told him.

"Jackie," he said very sadly. "What's up there that's so fascinating?"

"It's someone," she said.

"Jackie," he said. "There is no one in the attic."

"Yes, there is," Jackie answered, and she told her father and Mrs. Farquahrson about Frontrigo and the secret enchanted dress.

"This is nonsense," her father said.

"I'll show you," said Jackie.

They went to the steps. Mrs. Farquahrson sighed, looking doubtfully up the steep staircase.

"You wait here," Jackie's father said to her. "We'll be right back down. This won't take a minute."

He and Jackie climbed into the attic.

"You see," he said, "there's no one up here."

"You'll see," Jackie replied.

She went to the box and took out the dress.

"That was your mother's dress," her father said quietly. "When she was your age. Where did it come from? I've only seen it in pictures."

He watched with a strange look on his face as Jackie opened the buttons.

"If you hold my hand," she said, "I think it will work."

He did it. And they were back in the garden together. Her father looked about in amazement.

"You're back!" It was Frontrigo, who had come around the hedges.

Jackie introduced her father. Warily, Frontrigo and her father shook hands.

Frontrigo said, "Come, I invite you to a feast in my palace. Follow me!"

The palace was grand. There was an enormous chandelier in the front hall and the walls shined like gold. Two huge staircases rose before Jackie.

"There are three hundred stairs," Frontrigo boasted. He said he had counted them. Jackie asked if he didn't get tired, walking up and down. "No," said Frontrigo, "I'm quite used to it."

Jackie and her father were served a sumptuous meal. Afterwards Frontrigo said, "Come, I must give you a tour of the palace."

The palace was amazing. Frontrigo showed them everything. They even got to sit in the red velvet thrones of the King and the Queen.

"Comfy," Jackie's father said.

"Where's your room, Frontrigo?" Jackie asked.

Frontrigo did not have one room. He had many. There was a small throne in each one. He had a vast bed in one room, and another room full of paints and pictures. He also had an entire room where all the toys were made of glass—there were telescopes, periscopes and microscopes. There were kaleidoscopes and magical glasses, with little glass dolls decorating the frames. There were paperweights, in which snowstorms occurred when you shook the heavy balls upside down. Jackie especially liked the magical glasses and asked if she could try them on.

"My father did it once," said Frontrigo, "so I suppose you could, too."

"Are you sure this is okay, Frontrigo?" Jackie's father asked. He seemed bewildered by almost everything and had spoken very little.

"Of course," said Frontrigo.

When Jackie put on the glasses, she saw rainbows as bright as fireworks.

"My," she said. She gave the glasses back.

Frontrigo showed them to their rooms for the night. In the morning they found Frontrigo eating scones, which he shared with them. After breakfast, Jackie and Frontrigo went outside to play.

"Don't you have any swings?" Jackie asked.

"Many," said Frontrigo. Behind the palace there was an enormous park.

Jackie and Frontrigo had a wonderful day. They went to Frontrigo's apartments and tried on all his shoes. He had several hundred pairs. After that, Frontrigo showed Jackie the palace's orchards. There they picked a basket full of apricots. Frontrigo laid his coat on the grass and Jackie sat down on it. They ate apricots and drank buttermilk. Frontrigo picked some nuts from one of the bushes and threw them down for the squirrels.

After lunch, Frontrigo showed Jackie his boomerang. It was almost three feet long, and carved of ebony.

"Do you want to see me throw it?" They watched as it spun from his hand. "Whoops," said Frontrigo. "A little too high."

"Oh my," said Jackie. The boomerang was lost somewhere on the palace's steep, blue tile roof.

Frontrigo said one of the servants would get it. Jackie thought that it was lovely being a prince.

Frontrigo had many wonderful toys. Jackie's favorite was a small train which ran around the outside of the palace grounds. Frontrigo took her on a number of rides. He wore a blue striped cap and jerked the steam whistle. On the last turn around, he let Jackie pull the throttle.

Late in the afternoon, Jackie and Frontrigo took a short nap under the copper beech tree. When they woke up, Frontrigo told her about his plans for the evening. He wanted to build a large bonfire and roast dinner outside. He was the only child in the entire country, he told her. That was why he was so lonely. Thinking about that made Jackie sad. He said he would tell Jackie all about his mother and father, so she would know who they were if she saw them.

"Oh my," said Jackie for she remembered her father at that point and set out to find him. He was not far away. He was in the garden, amid the high hedges, sitting on a bench looking quite glum.

"What's wrong?" Jackie asked.

"I've been looking for your mother," he said. "I was certain I'd find her in this place. But she's not here. I've searched everywhere." Her father looked at Jackie. "We have to go home. I've missed work twice this week. This isn't a place for someone like me."

"But Dad, can't Frontrigo come with us?"

"If he likes," said her father. "And if he's allowed."

But Frontrigo could not go. He was a prince and the only child in the country. It was Jackie who had to stay, he explained.

"I told you," he said, "you can't just come and go from this place. You've left twice before. You promised you'd stay this time."

"But—" Jackie said.

"You promised," Frontrigo said again. Frontrigo tugged on Jackie's dress and begged her please. "If you leave this time," said Frontrigo, "you won't be able to come back."

Jackie looked at her father. He appeared quite sad.

"Jackie," he said, very quietly, and got to his feet. He touched her hand. "I can't stand to lose anyone else. You have to come with me."

Jackie knew that her father was right. She wrapped her arms around Frontrigo and told him good-bye. Frontrigo ran to the palace and came back with the magic glasses.

"I want you to have them. That way you'll remember me."

Jackie knew she would remember him anyway. But she took the glasses. Then she went with her father behind the hedge and started to take off the secret enchanted dress.

"Remember to hold my hands," she told her father.

He did. And they were back in their attic again. Jackie's father hugged her. They laughed and laughed when they heard Mrs. Farquahrson calling up the stairs.

The End.

"Hey Brian," I said, "how would you like to write a story with me?"

"Great," he said.

"It's for sort of a kids' book."

"Oh, uh-huh. Actually I'm trying to get in touch with my outer adult."

"I have an idea already," I said. "We can do kind of an update of the Sherlock Holmes thing about the dancing men."

"Cool. We'll make it an interstory."

"What's an interstory?"

"You know, like interactive. It involves giving the reader at least a couple of ways of making it come out."

"But don't they want to know what really happened?"

"What do you mean what *really* happened? It's fiction."

"But Brian, when I read a story, I want to feel as if it's really happening."

"This generation doesn't feel that way. I mean, they feel like if they help decide how it happens, it feels more like it's happening."

"Well, it—are you sure?"

"This is your son talking here."

"I'm aware of that."

"Trust me."

And I did.

Barbara D'Amato   Brian D'Amato

TOO VIOLENT

BY BARBARA D'AMATO
AND BRIAN D'AMATO

I'm an agent of the U.S. Treasury Department. My assignment was to find Kenny Logon and stick to him until he passed the four million dollars he was carrying to the mob.

We knew he hadn't been told beforehand where to go with it—the mob is too careful for that—so there was no way we could get there ahead of him. The overnight surveillance told me he was heading for O'Hare Airport.

This is it, I thought.

He had been spotted going into the airport video game arcade. I caught up with him there.

I hung back behind the Plexiglas partition, where he couldn't see me, and watched. There were a lot of kids around, and a few people in their twenties, like Kenny. He didn't talk to any of them. Nobody handed him a message. He walked around the arcade, as if looking for an interesting game. Then he grabbed one called Hands of Death, put a line of tokens on the side of the screen, grabbed the joystick, and played.

He played for forty-two minutes. I almost went over and grabbed him just because I was bored out of my mind, but it would have blown the whole case. At one point somebody else came up to try to play the game, but Kenny just stared him away with his gangster eyes. At another point he shifted his fanny pack and I could see that it was wired onto his body with a combination lock. I was feeling conspicuous out in the walkway so I strolled into the room and hung back in the darkest spot by the least-used pinball machine.

Suddenly, he turned away from the game and race-walked out the arcade door. I had been on the other side of the room, staying out of sight, I thought, but he knew he was being followed. Blast! I was just a little bit too far from Kenny; he was getting away.

I ran after him, just in time to see him slip into a crowd heading for the section that held Gates H1 through H30. I pushed through the crowd, bouncing off the stomach of an extremely overweight man, nearly overturning a baby carriage. A teenage girl dropped her bag of Gummi Fish when I rushed in front of her.

Kenny was gone. He was lost in a river of people heading all over the planet. I *had* to find him. I ran to the ticket agent at the nearest counter, flashed my ID card, and said I needed a list of all the planes leaving from those thirty gates.

"You mean the ones that are boarding now?" he asked.

"Yeah," I said. Kenny wouldn't be hanging around; he'd get on a plane at the last possible moment.

It seemed to take forever to print out the list:

SAN FRANCISCO

HONG KONG

LONDON

MINNEAPOLIS

MIAMI

PARIS

MANILA

SINGAPORE

NEW YORK

LOS ANGELES

ATLANTA

It was still too many planes to check individually. I was in trouble.

"Delay all the planes ten minutes," I told the agent. Any more and Kenny would probably get spooked. "Tell them the runway's tied up."

Desperate, I ran back to the arcade. He had to have gotten his message there, but how? I got tokens and put two in Hands of Death and played. Kick-boxing game. I got destroyed in the first two seconds by some big bruiser named Gort. There was no message there that I could see, but there had to be.

I'm too old for this stuff! I thought. *Kids understand these things; I don't.*

I looked around.

A girl of maybe nine or ten was entering her name, KIM, on the next game to the left. She was wearing black tights and a T-shirt with a picture of Barney the Educational Dinosaur eating kids.

CONGRATULATIONS, YOU ARE THE ALL-TIME HIGH-SCORER ON THIS MACHINE, said the words on the screen.

"Uh, excuse me, little girl?" I said.

"I am *not* 'little girl,'" she said. "You may call me sir."

"Uh, yeah, sir, excuse me, I'm with the FBI." I flashed my badge.

"I didn't do it," she said.

"I'm sure you didn't," I said. "You play these games a lot?"

"Sure. My mom says they're too violent. Do you think so?"

"Oh, certainly not," I said, "I think they're, uh, great. Do you know whether they change games often?" I was thinking, of course, that messages could be left by putting a doctored game in place.

"Sure they do. The best ones stay, though."

"You remember the man playing this game a couple of minutes ago?"

"Tall skinny guy with a butt pack? Dorkish hair?"

"Yeah, that's him."

"Uh-huh."

"Can you play this game for me and see if there's a message in it?"

"You are truly weird. But I'll play if you'll pay."

I handed her a stack of tokens and watched.

"Wow," she said. "Somebody named KEN got the last five high scores."

"That's the guy I'm looking for," I said.

"Hmm, there are only a few ways to get scores *this* high," she said. "You have to play as Stanley and fight Roc. That's this really baddest, lizardy-looking guy. And Stan's kind of a wuss. It's not easy."

"Do you think you could get the same scores?" I asked. The

mob might have just told him what scores to get, and somehow he'd learn from that where to go.

"Probably," she said. "I have a flight to Seattle in an hour, though, I'm playing in a Sonic the Hedgehog tournament there."

"Well, I'd be really happy if you could give it a try," I said. I wasn't cut out for this decade, I thought. Kim popped four tokens, chose Stanley, and started punching Roc:

SALUTATIONS.   BOX!

Then they knocked each other out:

HEAD BASH!   BOTH DOWN!

"*Ha!*" she said. "See, I tied it. Eight hundred and fifty million. I got it *exactly* right. I matched Kenny's last score!"

The two figures shook hands:

PERFECT TIE!

"Wow, you're incredible," I said.

She didn't argue with that. "Okay, let's try for the second score," she said.

The second fight went like this:

SALUTATIONS. UPPERCUT!   SPIN KICK!   ROC OUT!

Stanley raised his gloves over his head in a victory stance.

AWESOME!

"Creamed him," she said. "Okay, three more."

The next fight went on for a long time, but she stopped when she got to Kenny's score.

SALUTATIONS. ROC KICKS!   HEADLOCK!

Roc knocked out Stanley and stood in *his* victory stance.

TOSS!

ROC WINS!

"You realize I had to lose that one on purpose to match the score," she said.

"Of course," I said.

The next fight was a tie again and went like this:

SALUTATIONS. BOX!   HEAD BASH!   BOTH DOWN!   IT'S A TIE!

And the last one went like this:

SALUTATIONS. LEFT JAB!   BLOCK!   K.O.!   STAN WINS!

And it was over.

"Uh—sir," I said. "Is there a message?"

"Sure. You can't possibly have *missed* it! It's obvious."

DEAR READER: IF YOU ALREADY KNOW WHERE KENNY'S GOING, GO TO SECTION B. IF YOU NEED TO LOOK AT HIS MESSAGE AGAIN, GO TO SECTION A.

SECTION A

"Please," I said. "I'm just an adult. Tell me what it said."

She said, "Give me more money." I did. I looked at my watch. I had lost five minutes already.

She played it again, saying, "Now pay attention. Watch the freezes at the end of the action."

PERFECT TIE! AWESOME! ROC WINS! IT'S A TIE! STAN WINS!

"Miami!" I yelled. "The freeze-frame pictures at the end spell MIAMI."

"The older generation," she said, "is *so* slow!"

DEAR READER: PLEASE GO TO SECTION B.

SECTION B

I thanked her and ran out into the lobby toward the gates. The Miami flight was leaving in two minutes. If I really ran for it, I could make it.

I reached into my pocket for my badge and noticed there

was something in there that hadn't been there when I left home. I pulled it out and it was one of those origami birds, made out of folded blue paper.

I had a sneaking suspicion my young girl buddy had slipped it into my pocket while I was looking at the Hands of Death machine. I started to unfold it. I could see there was writing way down on the other side of the sheet, but it was so intricately folded that I didn't have time to stand there and undo it if I wanted to catch the plane.

DEAR READER: IF YOU WANT THE AGENT TO RUN FOR THE PLANE, PLEASE GO TO SECTION C. IF YOU WANT HIM TO TAKE THE TIME TO READ KIM'S NOTE, PLEASE GO TO SECTION D.

SECTION C

I was the last person to board the Miami flight. The aircraft door closed with a solid thud. We taxied to the runway. The plane took off and a minute later I heard the wheels fold up.

Now let's see where Kenny was.

I looked up the aisle, but didn't see him. Of course, from where I sat I couldn't see everybody aboard. I sat back to try to catch my breath. In a minute, I'd wander around and scope him out.

Kind of absent-mindedly, I put my hands in my pocket and found the origami bird. I unfolded it as delicately as possible— it took over a minute—and smoothed it out. The message was written to be read in a mirror. I held it up backward to the light from the window. It said:

SECTION D

It took me over two minutes to unfold Kim's note and figure out how to read it, but I still made the Paris flight with a whole three seconds to spare.

The 767 took off and a minute later I heard the wheels fold up. As we leveled off, I walked down the aisle, as though I was going to the bathroom. I felt this huge rush of excitement when I saw Kenny. Even better, he had earphones on and his eyes closed and there was a pink Post-it note sticking out of his jacket.

When I got even with Kenny, I pretended to lean down to look out the window of the seat behind him.

I may not be great at video games, but one thing I can do is pick pockets. I snagged the scrap of paper, palmed it, and walked on ahead to the bathroom and looked at the message. I held it up to the bathroom mirror.

Yes! Somebody had written Kenny a note about where to

meet his mob bagman. It had the place but not the city, because he wasn't told the city until he got to the airport. But it was a place every city had *one* of. I could phone ahead to Paris and have agents waiting. We'd see him pass the money and *we'd have him dead to rights!*

I looked at it again:

Maybe I'm not that dumb after all, I thought. And Kim was sneaky, but not *that* sneaky. I took out my notebook and wrote down the captions from underneath the freeze frames again, just so I could show it to my supervisor:

PERFECT TIE!   AWESOME!   ROC WINS!   IT'S A TIE!   STAN WINS!

P   A   R   I   S

Except for having to drop by the Bibliothèque Nationale tomorrow, this might be almost like a vacation.

I made a note to send Kim a chocolate Eiffel Tower.

We threw out the first story we outlined—funny, featuring kids, but a bit on the violent side. The trick was to come up with a story that would be suitable for kids, but interesting to adults and kids.

As a father of four (Stuart) and the eighteen-year-old baby-sitter to many (Lucy), we had a pretty good idea of the level a kid could relate to, if his or her intelligence and imagination weren't being underestimated.

We tried the basic story out on several kids in the age group this collection of stories is aimed for. No one had a problem with it and they all thought it was a good idea for a story.

The big surprise for both of us was that we could not only collaborate, but we could do it easily. Lucy wrote a draft. Stuart rewrote the draft. And we are both satisfied with the result.

Lucy is about to graduate from Oldfields School in Glencoe, Maryland, and she is looking forward to attending a college with a strong creative writing program. Among her favorite authors is Tobias Wolff—especially *This Boy's Life*—and two of her favorite books are *Alice in Wonderland* and *The Princess Bride*.

MOTHER KNOWS BEST

BY STUART KAMINSKY
AND LUCY KAMINSKY

Paul Banks looked out of his second-story window and into the street, watching his father pull away and his little brother playing kickball across the street with Patty Fergus.

It was the second date that his father had gone on in five years, since his parents' divorce. Paul had begged and pleaded with his father to allow him to watch his little brother by himself. At the age of twelve, he didn't need a baby-sitter watching him and Alex. Besides, he knew Alex better than anyone in the world. Paul's father had considered the argument for days. Finally, he'd given in.

As Paul's father had headed for the door, he had said to Paul, just as he had said so many times earlier that day, "And if your brother falls down in the street and gets run over by a car?"

"Go to Mrs. Fergus," Paul said.

"And if Alex won't go to bed and says he wants to watch Nick at Nite?"

"Smack him," Paul said, laughing.

But his father was not laughing as he adjusted his paisley tie for the umpteenth time and straightened out the arms of his jacket. He was very nervous about leaving his two boys home alone. He wasn't even terribly comfortable leaving them with a sitter.

"Paul—" he said.

"I know, I know. Tell him no garage sales tomorrow if he doesn't go to sleep on time," Paul reassured his father.

Finally, Paul almost had to push his father out of the door. Paul was home all alone. His brother was next door at Patty's house. Alex played with her far more than any of his other friends.

Lots of times Paul teased Alex about her with his Alex-has-a-girlfriend routine. Then Alex would get so frustrated that his ears would stick out and his nostrils would flare, and he would flail his fists at Paul, although this didn't accomplish anything. Paul always caught his little brother's arms, stopping his blows before they connected.

Paul turned away from the window and looked around the apartment thinking about what he was going to do next, now that he was all alone. He was happy that his father was dating again. He was afraid that his father spent too many nights thinking about his mother.

Paul hadn't seen his mother since the divorce. One day he had awakened and gotten out of bed and she was no longer there. When he went to breakfast that morning, his pretty blond mom in the terry cloth robe was not waiting in the kitchen, ready to fix him his scrambled eggs. As he left for school, she did not hand him his lunch money with a radiant smile. Instead, he got it himself.

Paul understood why his parents got the divorce. His

mother could be—well—difficult at times. She was pretty de-manding of his dad and Paul. She had a certain way of doing everything, and she wanted everyone else to do it her way, as well.

She liked the spices arranged in alphabetical order. She liked the fruits to go in the fruit drawer of the refrigerator, and the vegetables to go in the vegetable drawer. She liked clothes completely clean.

And if any of these things weren't the way she liked them—well—then she would fix them, or else get Paul's father or Paul to fix them. And if Paul didn't have time to get his grass stains out of his clothes because he had a baseball game or some-thing—well—then his mother would *make time* for him to do it. She was pretty forceful when she wanted to be.

Still, Paul loved his mother very much and missed her very much. She had a smell that only a mother has—one that a fa-ther cannot imitate. Sometimes Paul even smelled that scent on his friend Bill's mother when he went over to his house. And sometimes he wished that his mom were still living with them.

Paul seemed to remember, the night before she left, her coming into his bedroom in the middle of the night. He dimly remembered her giving him a kiss on the forehead, rubbing his hair behind his ears, and saying, "Don't worry, Paulie, I'll be back soon." Paul didn't really know if she actually did that, be-cause it was so late, and so long ago now, but he did know that she never came back. That was for sure.

Days, weeks, then months passed and finally Paul's father had said, after a Hamburger Helper dinner, that Paul's mother wouldn't be coming back. He told Paul that she had agreed his father would have sole and complete custody of Paul and his brother. Paul hadn't understood all that his father had told him, but he had taken it without crying, at least not till he got back to his room.

Paul walked away from the window and toward the back of the apartment to his room. Lying on his bed was a horror novel. He picked up the book and walked back into the living room.

Paul didn't really like the apartment that his father had chosen after the divorce. He hated its wood floors, and his room was way too small to share with his brother. Yet there was one place in the apartment where Paul actually felt comfortable— the window seat.

The apartment had a window facing the street, and edged into the wall was a window seat where Paul would sit. Sometimes he'd read a book, or look out at the traffic, or watch his brother play, or sometimes *just think*. Sometimes he would watch people walk in and out of the apartment building across from his.

Paul sat down in the seat and opened his book. He had just started it, and he always hated reading beginnings. They were so boring and time-consuming. Paul wished that books would just cut to the chase. Generally, Paul could plow through the beginning and then get to the interesting parts without any trouble. But today, Paul found the beginning of his book especially boring and couldn't make himself concentrate. Within five minutes he was looking out onto the street again.

Paul always told his little brother that he wished he would disappear, but now Paul wanted Alex's company. He felt kind of lonely, and a game of dominoes or Super Mario Brothers would have been kind of nice.

Maybe Alex would come back early. The door was open for him.

Paul looked at the large gray building across from his. An old woman was walking toward its main entrance, with a brown paper bag full of groceries in her arms, and a tiny yellow dog at her side. She got to the door and couldn't get her arms free to open it, but a woman came by to open it for her. The woman wore dark glasses and a straw hat. After she held the door open for the old woman, the woman in the straw hat walked across the street, heading toward Paul's building.

All that Paul could see now, as he looked down, was her brown straw hat, moving closer to his building. *Something about this woman is strange*, thought Paul. *She looks vaguely familiar.*

As she stepped even closer, Paul leaned over to get a better view. She glanced up and he got a good look at her face before she walked out of his sight and into his building. And then Paul realized what was so familiar about the woman. She looked a lot like his mother.

Paul jumped up from his seat and walked toward the door of the apartment. He opened it to see if she were coming to his floor. He didn't really believe that she was his mother, although he wished it was. But he didn't have anything else to do so he looked down the staircase and over the railing.

Paul saw the straw hat bobbing as the woman climbed the stairs. But as she moved closer, Paul realized that it was rude to stare at her. Certainly the woman was not his mother, he decided, and he tried to run back to his apartment before she saw him.

But it was too late. The woman had seen Paul.

She ran up the last few steps and met him at the door. Paul felt ashamed. He was getting ready to apologize and say that he had mistaken her for someone else when she removed her sunglasses and took a good hard look at him.

"Paulie," she said. Paul couldn't believe her lips had formed his name.

Indeed, the woman in the brown straw hat and sunglasses *was* his mother.

"Look, Paulie. It's me. I've come back to visit," she said with a smile. She took off her brown straw hat and was now holding it in her hands, in front of her. She rumpled up her blond hair so that Paul could recognize her.

"Mom?" Paul asked. He didn't really remember his mother too well. He was so young when she had left. She was the same, but different. Still tall, still pretty, but not young-looking anymore. She seemed as if she were working hard at looking happy.

And her breath smelled funny, like when Dad had a beer at night. Now it came back to him. That smell had been part of her too before she had left.

"Saw your daddy leave," she said. "I didn't think he'd be too glad to see me. Where's Alex?"

"Out," said Paul. "He'll be home later."

"That's all right. Let's go inside. I came to see how my boys are doing."

When they were inside, Paul turned to his mother. The smell he remembered was still there. So was the pain of her leaving.

"What are you doing here?" Paul asked. He didn't want to sound rude, but it was the first thing that came into his head when he saw her. It had been five years.

"Well, that's hardly the welcoming that I was hoping for. I was shooting for something along the lines of 'Hi, Mom' and maybe a hug. How 'bout it, kiddo?" his mother asked.

Paul hesitated, taking another good look at her before he went into her arms. He clasped his arms around her waist, and the old smell, that old motherly smell, came back to him again even stronger. And with it came memories, because he smelled that other thing on her breath.

"I've missed you, baby," she said. "I hardly remember little Alex, but I miss him and the way he smelled and baby-smiled."

As they finished hugging, Paul began to have doubts. What did she want from them, now that she had already been gone all this time? Why hadn't she called them—at least Alex—on Christmas and on their birthdays? And what was she doing here, now that their father was out?

"Mom, why didn't you call?" Paul asked.

"Well, I figured you would ask that and you have every right to. Why don't we just sit here and talk? We have so much catching up to do," his mother said.

Paul folded his arms and tried to look mature and stern. "Where were you? Why didn't you ever call?"

"Oh, Paul, don't look so sour. Come and have a seat with me and I'll explain everything," Paul's mother said. She had now seated herself upon their large beige living-room couch, and she was patting the seat beside her, suggesting that Paul sit there.

Paul came around to sit with his mother. He still tried to keep his expression as stern as possible and to show little emotion or happiness at her return until she got to some explaining.

"Well...?" Paul said.

Paul's mother took a deep breath and began.

"I know you have questions and I understand. It's like this: I had a problem. Do you know what alcoholism is?"

He nodded. "I think so."

"Well, it got worse and worse. I don't know why I had it or where it came from. Doctors had all kinds of ideas for treatments. I even tried something called AA, Alcoholics Anonymous. But...do you understand?"

"I think so," said Paul.

"I wrote to you, sometimes every week, but I never got an answer. I thought you were just too angry with me for leaving to answer. Well, a few months ago, I decided that my problem was almost gone so I looked for you and your father and brother. But you were gone. The company your father worked for was out of business. He hadn't left a forwarding address. I realized you hadn't gotten any of my letters. I didn't know where you were. Now I work as a teller in Nationwide Bank in Tennessee. I really have my life together now, and I feel so much better," his mother said. She looked at Paul as if she were desperate for his understanding. "Then, one day, an old friend came in and said you guys had moved here."

Paul's mother didn't look like a bank teller to him. She looked like a woman pretending that everything was all right when it wasn't. She did a bad job of pretending.

"I still don't understand why you didn't call us, and why you showed up here now, anyway," Paul said. *Don't give in until you get your answers*, he told himself.

"Paul, your father has sole custody of you and your brother because of my problem. I really should have talked to him about this first, but I didn't know if... Look, I came five hundred miles, practically across the country to see you and your brother and I was hoping for something a little more. Where is your brother?" she asked. She moved her head, looking around the apartment for Alex.

"I told you. He's out," Paul said. He didn't want her to know where Alex was. If she knew, and she went to get him, it might upset Alex. After all, Paul was responsible for his brother. He didn't want his mother to see Alex until she explained herself more clearly, and he could figure out the odd way she was behaving.

"Oh. Well—I was hoping to see him, too. This just ruins everything," his mother said. Her pretty face drooped and she sunk her head in her hands for a moment.

"Ruins what?" Paul asked. He was beginning to get irritated

with her and he wanted his answers—and wanted them now. "What are you doing here, anyway? You should come back when Dad's here."

She laughed, but it was a secret laugh.

"There's a court ruling against me coming near you and your brother," she said. "I'm not even supposed to be in this state, and I'm never supposed to drive again. But don't worry, I've got a car parked around the corner. My lawyers and doctors say I'm well enough to go back to court and get at least some visiting rights. I just couldn't wait."

"I don't understand," said Paul.

"The accident," she said, leaning forward and looking into his eyes for a sign of remembrance. "The night before I was supposed to check into a treatment center, I got you and your brother out of bed. Your father was working late, and we went for a ride in the car. I crashed. Judge said I had been driving on a revoked license, said I was drinking. I admitted that I couldn't stop. The judge said I needed help. The doctor said I could come back with someone, pack my things, and say good-bye to you. After six months of different treatments, I wasn't making much progress, and your father divorced me. I couldn't blame him. I didn't fight him. Those first three years were a kind of blur, Paulie. And then I started feeling better."

"Accident?" asked Paul. "You said there was an accident in the car when I was little."

"Nobody was hurt. And now, I'm ready to take you kids back. So what do you say? How would you like to come with me to Tennessee? I realize this is a little sudden, but I have to get back to work on Monday, and I'd like you kids to come with me. So?" his mother asked, trying to sound casual, as if she were asking Paul about the weather.

"I think you should talk to Dad before we go anywhere." Paul said. It was strange, but now that she was so near, it was all coming into focus. He suddenly remembered the accident, and he knew what happened to him because of it.

"I'll talk to him. I'll convince him, if you boys want to. Do you?"

Her eyes were wet now as if she were going to cry.

Paul felt as if he were being pushed into a tight corner, and he thought his mother had been drinking. He watched enough television to know that, and had seen old Mr. Howard upstairs come in after he had been drinking.

"Are you drunk?" he asked.

"No," she said, shaking her head emphatically. "I had a single drink before I came here. I'm nervous, Paulie. You can understand that?"

Paul couldn't understand. Why had she let herself get sick in the first place? Why had she put them in the car that night? And why hadn't she made herself get better faster?

She doesn't even know what happened to me, Paul realized. Hadn't the doctors told her? Hadn't Paul's father?

"How could I just leave Dad alone?" Paul asked. "I mean, why should I?"

"Why should you, Paulie? Is that what you want to know? Well, for starters, because I'm your mother. I know you better than anyone else—and better than your father ever will. I gave birth to you. I felt you inside me," she said.

"Well, you just shove in here after all this time and say that you know so much about me. What do you know? What can you know about me, since you haven't even seen me for half of my life?" Paul asked. He was starting to get angry. How dare she? He got up from the couch and was now standing in front of her. He did not want to get comfortable with her. He had to stay in control.

Secretly, though, Paul was very afraid. His father was gone and he was in charge. And now his mother was in front of him, asking him questions and forcing him to make decisions, just like an adult.

"What do I know about you, Paul? Well, the list could just go on for days. I realize that I left you for a long time, but remember, before that I took care of you every single day while your father was off at work and God knows where else," she said. She looked away and put her head in her hands again and then looked up at her son.

"If you know so much about me," said Paul, "then tell me. What do you know about me that Dad doesn't? And why should I come with you?"

"All right," his mother said. "I can see why you're irritated with me. You have every right. Now just come back and sit down and let's talk this out. I hadn't intended to ask you to come with me so soon. I just wanted to talk. It's just that I was so excited to see you that I couldn't help myself."

Paul began to feel a little bit sorry for his mother. She had come so far to see him, and she hadn't meant to be gone for so long, hadn't meant to do what she had done. He decided that he would at least hear her out, before he made any decisions.

"Okay, Paulie, you want to know what I know about you, right? Well—I remember odd things about you. But here's some proof that I know you. You have a tiny brown birthmark in the center of your chest. Your favorite ice cream is—or at least was—mint chocolate chip. You hate the color purple. Is that enough proof?" his mother asked. Exasperated, she leaned forward and looked into Paul's eyes.

"Sure, you know little things about me, but what do you *really* know about me? How could you know me, after all this time?" he asked.

"I know more than you think I do. Really, Paul. Do we have to go through this? Can't we talk about other, more important things? Where is your brother, anyway?" she pleaded, looking first at her watch and then at the door.

"I told you, Alex is away—and now can you please answer my questions?" Paul asked. He wanted to know. He needed to know what his mother knew, her special reasons why he should just pack up and leave everything.

"All right. Okay. But after this, I'd like to stop all this nonsense. I need to know whether you're coming or not," she said. "There isn't really much time. Okay. You never cared for knock-knock jokes. You hate asparagus. You love to read comic books, science fiction, and horror. Your favorite television show is 'Star Trek.' And when you sneeze, you sneeze in fits of twenty or thirty sneezes." She sat back in the couch and looked at Paul as if to say, "Your turn."

Everything that Paul's mother had said about him was true, down to the last detail. Paul's father was bad with details about his sons. He loved them, played with them when he wasn't working, took them to movies and the zoo, but he didn't remember these little things. But Paul was not going to give in to his mother just because she knew a couple of strange details about him. Not after all this time.

"Look, Mom, I can't leave Dad. That's all there is to it. I just don't see why, after all this time, I should go with you. I don't even know if you love me," Paul said. And then he knew what was coming.

"Of course I love you. Probably more than your father ever did. Don't you see? All of these years I have been planning to have a life with you and Alex. I wanted things to go right. Paulie, I know you better than anyone. Haven't I shown you that? I need you, Paul, and you need me, and that's just all there is to it."

Paul's mother now stood up and moved in front of him. Her pretty face had turned pink and she was clearly beginning to get extremely frustrated.

"Shouldn't you talk to your doctor and lawyer and Dad before we go anywhere with you?" he asked.

"I've explained that," she said in a pleading voice. "Now, please, please let's pack for you and Alex and pick him up wherever he is."

Paul was not going with her. He tried to ease the determined expression on his face and to think of how to tell her this. He didn't want to upset her even more. Even after all of the pains that she had caused him, he didn't want to hurt her. She looked so frightened and she kept reaching out just to touch her son. Paul took a deep breath before opening his mouth.

"Look, Mom. You're gonna have to leave. Dad doesn't know you're here, and I can't make all of these decisions now. Please, can't you come back later?" Paul asked. He tried to say all of this as lightly as he could.

"No," she said, standing up. "It has to be now. If it's not now... A child is supposed to be with his mother, to live with his mother. That's how God intended it, and—"

Just then, as Paul's heart jumped somewhere into his throat, his mother said, "Well?"

"Well, what?"

"Answer the phone."

Paul hadn't heard it ring.

"If it's your brother, tell him to come home now, quickly. If it's your father, tell him everything is fine. Please don't tell him I'm here."

Paul carefully walked to the phone with his mother close behind him. He slowly picked up the receiver.

"Hello," Paul said.

Paul's mother was standing next to him, her ear pressed to the receiver right next to her son's. As she listened, she clamped one hand hard onto Paul's shoulder. Then she cupped her other hand over the bottom of the receiver.

"Paulie, tell your father everything is fine. Now. Do it," said his mother. She stared pleadingly into Paul's eyes. She looked very serious, very determined.

"Everything is fine, Dad," Paul said into the receiver.

Paul's mother listened by the phone once more, then looked straight at Paul.

"Tell him that everything is fine, again," she said.

"Everything is fine, Dad," Paul said, again. "Alex should be home soon. I'm just listening to my CD and reading."

His mother listened once more, then said, "Tell him 'okay.'"

"Okay," Paul said. "I won't stay up late listening. I'll take care of Alex. Stay out as long as you like. Have fun."

"Say good-bye," Paul's mother said to Paul, still looking into his eyes forcefully. "Please."

"Good-bye," Paul said, and then his mother grabbed the receiver and hung up.

"Now," she said, "I didn't mean to get so harsh, but you just have to listen to me. I know what's best for you, Paulie—for Alex, for me. You have to come with me. That's all there is to it. I know you better than anyone else."

Paul was now scared to death. His pulse pounded and his stomach churned. He felt that he had better pay attention. He prayed that Alex would not walk in now.

"I want you to show me to your room so that we can get your bags ready to go. I'll call your father in the morning from Nashville and everything will work out fine." She smiled at him. Paul nodded. He realized that she was going to force him to do whatever she said. She had made up her mind long before she had walked through his door and there was no changing it, no matter what.

He looked at the clock. Almost seven. Alex would be coming in soon.

With his heart still pounding, Paul led his mother across the living room and toward his bedroom. As he walked through the hall, he passed a picture of him and Alex and his father taken in a small booth at a mall. He told himself to be strong.

As they walked into Paul's bedroom, his mother looked around.

"Nice poster," she said, pointing to a poster of a tyrannosaur that Paul had bought at the science museum.

Paul looked at her.

"You got a suitcase?" she asked.

Paul nodded, then bent down and dragged a gray paisley suitcase from under the bed. He wanted to do things as slowly as possible. He took his time placing the suitcase on the bed and opening it. He had to stall.

"Pack enough for you and your brother. We can buy more in Nashville. Just pack fast," she said.

"Look, Paul," she continued after a few moments, "I hadn't meant to be so harsh with the phone call from your father. But right now I don't think you realize what's for your own good. I'm ready to take you back, and I won't hurt you again. I've planned all of these years to be with you guys."

His mother was sitting on Alex's bed with her legs crossed in front of her while he slowly packed, not thinking about what he was putting into the suitcase. She looked at the pattern of red and green and blue cars on Alex's comforter, and fluffed up his pillow nervously.

"It'll be fun. You like McDonald's? We'll stop there," she said.

Paul didn't answer his mother. He didn't even look at her. But he did remember the way she used to be: her soft, slow, gentle but determined voice, a voice that was not to be denied even when he was seven.

"Hurry up," she said, looking at her watch. "All you need to pack are the necessities—toothbrush, toothpaste, you know. We'll call your father later and he can send the rest. When you finish, we can go get Alex. We can't wait around here, baby."

She was now walking around Paul's room, examining every little thing. She picked up Paul's baseball trophy from the past year and examined it.

Paul walked across the room to his dresser drawer. He would not say anything to his mother, he decided. He would just do this all as slowly as possible. He did not want his mother to even have the chance to see Alex. Lord knew how Alex would react to this.

Paul took out shorts, shirts, and underwear and put them into his suitcase. He walked back across the room and got his socks. He put them into the suitcase as well.

"Oh, Paulie. I'm so excited. We're all going to be together again. I just can't wait to show you around the city. I know you, and I know you'll like it," she said.

She went on talking and talking, but Paul paid no attention. Instead, he slowly packed his clothes, his books, and other things he really didn't need.

Paul didn't know how much time had passed when his

mother sprang up from Alex's bed in alarm. She looked toward the living room as if she'd heard a noise. Paul checked his watch. It had only been ten minutes since the call from his father. *It must be Alex*, thought Paul.

"Who is that?" asked his mother, moving toward the door. "Is that you, Alex?"

Both Paul and his mother rushed to the living room. Paul prayed as he walked down the hall, prayed that it wasn't his brother, prayed as he had prayed with his father at his side in the hospital five years earlier. When he moved into the living room a step behind his mother, he realized that his prayer had been answered.

In front of him in the living room was his father, who was holding Alex's hand. And a policeman stood beside them.

Paul rushed to his father's side and took his father's other hand. He had never been so happy to see his father in his whole life.

"Beth, what are you doing here?" Paul's father asked.

"I've come to see my sons, Jim, is that such a crime?" she asked.

Paul looked at Alex, who said, "Is that my mother?"

Paul nodded yes.

"I think I know what you're doing here," Paul's father said, looking past her into the boys' room and seeing the half-full suitcase on his son's bed. "Beth, this isn't the way."

"It's not what you think," Paul's mother said to his father.

"You were trying to take Paul and Alex," Paul's father said.

"Well, why shouldn't I? They're my sons. I deserve them. I

know them better than you ever will," she said. "I know them in here," she said, pointing to her heart.

"You're not supposed to come anywhere near them, Beth," Paul's father said. "You're supposed to see your lawyer. We can work something out, but not this way."

Just then the policeman cleared his throat and said, "All right, folks. We can talk this out later. Ma'am, you're gonna have to come with me. I'm gonna escort you out. We're gonna have to file a little report because of this." He walked across the room and put his hand on Paul's mother's back, urging her toward the door.

"For what? What have I done?" Paul's mother asked.

"We'll talk about that at the station," the officer said.

"I'll get someone to stay with the boys and then I'll be right there, Officer," Paul's father said.

"I don't understand," said Paul's mother. "Paul told you that you could stay out late. Why did you come back? Why did you bring the police?"

"Paul answered the phone," his father said. "He answered the phone and said he was spending a quiet evening listening to his CD."

"So?" she said.

"Paul's deaf, Beth. When you had the car crash, Paul's hearing was damaged. He was deaf within a year. He learned to read lips."

Then the policeman and Paul's mother left the apartment.

As Paul's mother walked down the stairs with the officer, however, she remained confused.

"Well, I never knew that about Paul," his mother said. "I never knew that about him."

"I guess you don't know him as well as you think you do," the officer said.

And then the officer escorted Paul's mother out of Paul's building and to the police station.

My daughter Christina took dance lessons for five years when she was growing up, and was gifted enough to be invited into the "Talent Class" at the studio, proof positive that genes aren't everything. My only formal instruction was a disco class in the late seventies—that craze ended soon after. A coincidence? I think not.

Nevertheless, we both have fond memories of tap shoes and jetés, so when we put our heads together via long distance, a dance studio seemed a natural setting. Christina supplied the terminology and atmosphere, and suggested that the mystery center on a missing mascot or pet. For the record, our first choice was a hamster, but as a rule rodents do not inspire warm feelings…and they don't talk.

I relied on memories of the way Christina spoke when she was ten for most of the dialogue. Belfry was named for a lovebird in her menagerie, and her favorite teacher's name is Stark.

I supplied the young detective, Sydney, who appears here in her first case, at the age of ten. Sydney Bryant is a series character who is dear to my heart, and I was intrigued by the idea of writing about her as a child.

The rest was fun…and never mind the phone bill.

Patricia Wallace   Christina Wallace

RELEVÉ

BY PATRICIA WALLACE
AND CHRISTINA WALLACE

"Keep your back straight, Sydney."

At the barre, Sydney straightened her back and made a face at her own reflection in the mirror. A simple thing, unless you had to keep your balance while standing with your heels touching and your toes pointed outward in opposite directions—

"Second position," Miss Stark said, cheerily. "Very nice, girls...remember to keep your back straight, head up, tummy in, and chest out."

With only a slight wobble, Sydney managed a plié into the second position, and cast an envious glance at Clarice, whose graceful knee bend seemed as effortless as breathing. At eleven, Clarice was only a year older than she, but Clarice had been taking dance lessons for a lot longer than six months— and it showed.

"Nice, very nice," Miss Stark said. "Third position, now, shall we?"

"Relevé," Belfry squawked from his perch in the corner. "On your toes!"

"Hush, Belfry, *I'm* teaching this class, thank you very much." All the same, Miss Stark crossed the studio/garage and handed the green-and-yellow parrot an apple slice. He promptly tossed it on the floor. "Mind your manners, will you, please?" said Miss Stark.

In response, Belfry gave a wolf whistle, which set the neighborhood dogs to barking.

Sydney laughed along with the other girls, but held her position, not wanting to have to start over. If they didn't get through the lesson, Miss Stark might make them stay late, and she was anxious to get home.

She wanted to read a few chapters of *The Mirror Crack'd* before dinner; it was her ambition to be a detective when she grew up and—

"Back to work, girls," Miss Stark said crisply. "If we get to our jazz steps by four o'clock, we can take a break for ice cream before tap."

Which they did, walking the two blocks to Murphy's Market on the corner of Elm and Pacific. Most of the girls had changed into their tap shoes—which they really weren't supposed to wear outside—and they shuffle-stepped all the way.

It was warm, still, although the afternoon sun was low in the sky. Southern California was like that, even three weeks before Christmas.

Nevertheless, Sydney admired the decorations in the front windows of the houses they passed. Snow sprayed in swirling patterns, big red-and-white candy canes, and cutout reindeer pulling Santa in his sleigh. A couple of houses had trees by the windows, dripping foil "icicles" and strung with colored lights.

Only one house on the block wasn't decorated, and that

was the Porters'. Their bay window revealed only a deep, wide basket full of pussy willows, its attached lid hanging to one side. Mrs. Porter probably didn't feel much like celebrating Christmas, since her husband had died this past summer and she was in mourning. An older couple, they hadn't had any kids, so it was just her, alone.

As often as not, Mrs. Porter would be standing by the window, looking out, when Sydney passed on her way home from dance class. Mrs. Porter did a lot of that, looking out. But not today, although the drape was stirring—

Ahead, Miss Stark ushered the girls into a single file, making space on the sidewalk for a man who wasn't walking exactly straight.

Sydney regarded him with some interest. He was wearing a long gray coat and darker gray corduroy pants. His black high-top tennis shoes weren't laced up all the way, and the tongues flapped as he walked. Unshaven, with his hair sticking up in little peaks, and watery pale blue eyes, he looked kind of suspicious, like a character out of one of her father's *True Detective* magazines.

"Sydney," Miss Stark called from the front of the line, "come along now."

Recognizing the note of caution in her dance teacher's voice, she hurried to catch up, with one last glance over her shoulder.

Back at the studio, fifteen minutes later, she and the other girls were in position, holding a pose in front of the mirror. They

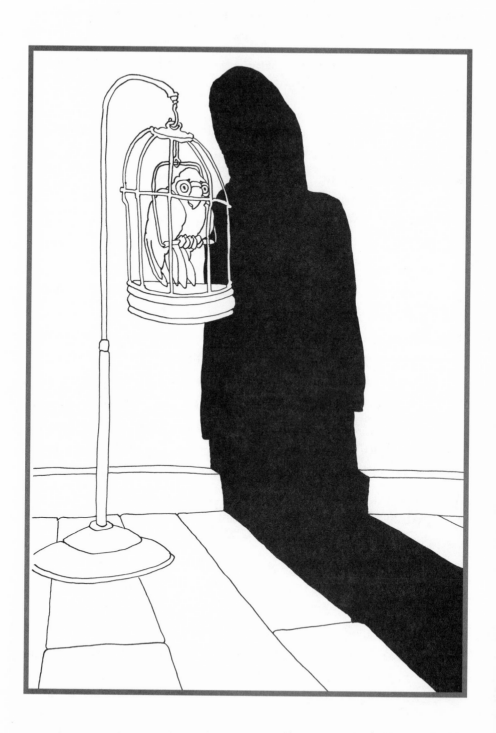

were waiting for the music cue to begin their tap routine, when Miss Stark let out a startled cry.

"Belfry!"

For a heartbeat, there was only the quiet hiss of the record player, which then faded as the familiar melody of "You Are My Sunshine" began to play.

No one bothered to dance, not even Clarice.

Turning from the mirror, Sydney saw that the door to Belfry's cage was open, his perch empty. She started over, her taps clattering, at the same time scanning the room for any sign of the parrot. Not that there was anywhere for him to hide; the wood floor was bare, and all of their ballet cases had been stashed in cubbyholes that were built into the wall above a long bench.

Miss Stark was simply standing, her hands covering all of her face except her eyes.

Sydney reached the cage first—she might not be graceful but she *was* fast—and glanced in. Belfry's food and water dishes were undisturbed, and there was clean newspaper on the bottom of the cage, advertising a two-passenger Gremlin for $1,879.

A single, clipped feather lay on the newspaper. It was mostly green, but edged with dark blue.

"Has he gotten out before?" Rosemarie asked.

"Maybe he flew away." Clarice had gone over to the lone window in the studio, but it was cranked open only an inch or two. "Maybe he'll come back."

"He's a parrot, not a homing pigeon," Lisa offered, pushing

her glasses up with one finger. "They don't have the instincts to find their way home."

"Then we should go and look for him. How far can a parrot fly?"

"He can't fly at all," Sydney said matter-of-factly. She showed them the feather and ran her fingertip over the squared tip. "This came from Belfry's wing, because only flight feathers are clipped this way."

"That's right," Miss Stark murmured, reaching for the feather and then brushing it ever so lightly against her flushed cheek.

"Then…where is he?" Clarice asked.

Angela, who almost never said anything, added, "And how did he get out?"

"Someone took him," Miss Stark said, a bleak expression on her face.

Having suspected that from the beginning, Sydney merely nodded in agreement.

"The door was unlocked. I've lived in this neighborhood for twenty-two years. I've never had to lock my doors…and now this."

Sydney did the arithmetic and arrived at 1948, the same year, coincidentally, that her parents had moved here.

Her father was always saying how much the neighborhood—and all of San Diego—had changed since then.

"Poor Belfry," Rosemarie said.

"That man," Clarice said, excitedly. "That man we saw on the way to get ice cream—"

"*He* doesn't live around here," Lisa said. "Maybe he took Belfry—"

Why would he? Sydney wondered.

"Call the police," Molly suggested, bouncing from foot to foot.

"No, girls," Miss Stark said with a sigh, tucking Belfry's feather into the pocket of her skirt. "The police are very busy. They wouldn't have time to search for a lost bird."

But a private detective might.

At home that evening, after dinner, Sydney went into the living room, where her father was reading, as he did every night after dinner, in his overstuffed chair. Smoke from his pipe drifted up to the ceiling, and as she climbed onto the wide, cushioned arm of the chair, she waved her hand through it. Although she loved the smell of his cherry tobacco, she didn't like the actual smoke.

"Dad?"

"What is it, honey?" her father asked without looking up from the paper.

Sydney wrapped her arms around her knees and hugged them to her chest. "Why would anyone steal a parrot?"

A smile tugged at the corner of his mouth, causing a jiggle in the stream of smoke. "I don't know. Are there any pirates in town?"

"Daaad…"

"No? Well, then, let me think." He folded the paper and put it aside, then cupped his chin in his hand and gazed upward, as though he were thinking hard. After a moment, he shook his head. "I must admit, I don't know, punkin. What do you think?"

He was always doing that, turning her questions back to her, so she was ready with a backup question. "Okay, then how much does a parrot cost?"

"Whew." Her father ran his hand through his hair. "These days everything's expensive—"

"You can get a Gremlin for $1,879," Sydney said, recalling the ad she'd seen. Her father had told her many times, being a detective was in the details, and you never knew what might be important.

"And worth every penny, I'm sure," he said, eyebrows raised. "But the minimum wage is a dollar and sixty cents an hour, my darling daughter, which is more to the point. I'd guess a parrot is an exotic bird, so we're probably talking maybe eighty dollars—"

"Eighty dollars?" She had saved her allowance all year so she could buy Christmas presents, and she had only thirty-two dollars and seventy-five cents.

"—to a hundred, depending on whether the bird can talk and how old it is."

In her mind, Sydney heard Belfry's odd little voice. *On your toes!*

"Then again, times are tough, and I imagine you could sell a bird like that." His pipe had gone out, and he busied himself for a moment, striking a match, huffing like the Little Engine That Could. "Why do you ask, punkin?"

Sydney told him everything, from the man on the street to

the feather to Miss Stark not wanting to call the police to look for whoever took Belfry.

"Hmm," he said when she finished. "Quite the puzzle, isn't it?"

"The thing is, how did the man even know Belfry was in the studio to steal? No one can see in, and it's—" Sydney paused to think of the word, "soundproof so the music won't bother anyone."

In the kitchen, the phone rang twice before her mother answered it.

Her father smiled but shook his head. "I'm sure there's a logical reason—"

"Jonathan," her mother called, "telephone."

"Keep thinking," he said as he got up from the chair. On the way out, he leaned over and kissed the top of her head. "It'll come to you."

Sydney took his place, sinking into the cushions and closing her eyes.

It did not come to her, not then.

On Friday, she had dance class after school. As she made her way over to Miss Stark's studio, she noticed that the dogs were barking for some reason. There was no one else besides her on the street, and the dogs never barked at the kids who lived in the neighborhood.

That's strange, Sydney thought, but she had other things to think about, and so forgot it.

At the studio, she felt drawn to the black wrought-iron cage. But when she went over to it, the cage was empty, its door standing open. The food and water dishes had been removed, as had the newspaper.

Belfry had not returned.

Sydney closed the little door and frowned. She went over to the bench and sat down to change into her ballet slippers. The other girls were already at the barre, warming up with stretching exercises.

Miss Stark appeared in the doorway with a smile on her face, although her eyes were kind of puffy and red, as though she'd been crying.

"Good afternoon, girls," Miss Stark said brightly. As always at the start of every class, she twirled several times, her skirt billowing out in a shimmery circle around her. "Shall we dance?"

"Yes, Miss Stark," the others said.

Sydney had only one slipper on when the music started, and she hopped to the barre, pulling the second slipper over her heel.

"Up, Up and Away" was playing loudly, but no one was dancing except for Miss Stark. And *she* acted as if she'd forgotten they were there, doing one lovely pirouette after another, which was far too advanced for their class.

It struck Sydney then, from out of the blue. "Oh," she said, then ran to the door, went out, and closed it behind her.

She couldn't hear the music.

But the dogs had heard Belfry on Wednesday. Dogs could

hear better than humans, she knew, and they had barked after the parrot whistled.

They were barking now.

Relevé. On your toes!

Sydney blinked, startled. Could it be that Belfry was nearby and the dogs were hearing him? If so, if she listened really hard, maybe she'd hear him, too.

All else forgotten, Sydney headed down the street in her ballet slippers, leotard, and tights.

She was almost to the market when she remembered the basket in the Porters' bay window. Had it been there when she passed the house a minute ago?

A basket with an attached lid, just the thing to put a parrot in and whisk it away. The drape had been stirring in the window...Had Mrs. Porter been watching as they left the studio?

Being a detective was in the details. She hadn't believed the man on the street that day could have known about Belfry in the first place, but of course Mrs. Porter would know.

Sydney turned and walked slowly back to check, with a kind of funny, fluttery feeling in her stomach.

The basket was gone from the window.

Her heart beat a little faster as she followed the winding path up to the front porch. She could see into the living room, neat as a pin, as her mother would say, only every bit as empty as Belfry's cage had been...

Sydney thought about how lonely her mother would feel if something happened to her father, and maybe she had never been born. *Their* house, with empty rooms and no one to talk to. It hurt to even think about it.

With her ear to the door, Sydney heard a familiar muffled squawk from the back of the house.

"Step together, step together, shuffle step," Belfry directed. "On your toes! Relevé!"

Sydney smiled. He was forever mixing up ballet and tap moves. Her smile faded, though, when she heard Mrs. Porter's delighted laughter.

"On my toes, indeed," Mrs. Porter said. "I have work to do, my fine feathered friend. You'd best let me get to it if you want these walnuts and filberts shelled for your supper."

The fluttery feeling in her stomach had turned into an ache. She was glad to have found Belfry safe and sound, but wasn't looking forward to asking Mrs. Porter if she had, by chance, seen Miss Stark's lost parrot.

The way she saw it, she *had* to ask. Even though Mrs. Porter would probably be sad not to have someone to talk to, living alone the way she did, Belfry belonged to Miss Stark. And Miss Stark missed him.

Sydney took a deep breath and rang the bell.

That Sunday afternoon, she had her dad drive her to Mrs. Porter's house. Balanced on her knees was a small cage, covered by a drape to keep the birds calm and quiet.

Sydney peeked into the cage. She had chosen the white lovebirds at the pet store because they seemed to like each other. They also did a kind of dance, bobbing their heads up and down as they spread their wings.

"Do you think Mrs. Porter will like them? I mean, they don't talk or anything." At last report, Belfry hadn't *stopped* talking since being returned to Miss Stark and his own comfy cage two days ago.

"I'm sure she will, honey," her father said, pulling over to the curb.

Judging by the look on Mrs. Porter's face when she answered the doorbell a minute later, her father was right. Mrs. Porter's smile was worth every penny of Sydney's Christmas money.

As for the rest of it, no one needed to know what Mrs. Porter had done; it was their secret. After all, a private detective needed to be discreet.

When I proposed the collaboration to my daughter Nicole, she immediately said, "A cat should be the hero."

We always had cats while she was growing up (we both still do)—we even had a cat named Moxie, so that was a natural. Though we live less than ten miles apart, we both have insanely busy schedules, so we spent a few evenings on the telephone and one long morning languishing in a deserted coffee shop drinking chocolate coffee and making notes.

It was a fun, creative endeavor, a good opportunity to get together to do something different. We work well together. Perhaps we'll do it again.

MOXIE AND THE AFRICAN QUEEN

BY ELIZABETH ENGSTROM
AND NICOLE ENGSTROM FOURMYLE

Moxie couldn't wait for Sandra to go to work so he could investigate the new arrival. It sat quietly, mysteriously, on *his* windowsill, singing softly to itself. It drove Mox crazy with curiosity. It was hard for him to be patient.

Sandra hated it when he played with the plants, so he had to wait until she went to work. But as soon as she left, Mox and his friends would play. They played and laughed and giggled and had a good time. All day long. Until naptime, of course. Then Mox would curl up in his favorite sunbeam on his favorite windowsill, and let his thick gray fur soak up the warmth.

But now there was a newcomer on *his* windowsill. How could Sandra do that? That windowsill was his personal place.

Sandra kept a lot of plants in the apartment. There was Wakefield-Smith, the Boston fern. He tantalized Mox with his tentacle-like fronds that were just out of reach, even when Mox stood up on the table.

There was Magnolia, the ficus tree that stood in the corner. She was very fragile. She was rarely in a good mood; most of the time she whined. Mox only had to look at her as if he'd like to climb her spindly little branches and all her leaves would fall off. He teased her sometimes, but he could tell she didn't like it very much. He only did it when he was really, really bored.

Lucas and Joseph, two poinsettias that had been in the apartment since Christmas, were on a stand in the corner. They pretty much kept to themselves, just changing colors and whispering to each other in some foreign language. They spoke Hawaiian, Wakefield-Smith said.

A whole shelf next to the stereo was filled with squat little planters lined up in a row, and in each one was a different kind of fat plant covered with prickly stickers. They weren't any fun at all. They didn't laugh, they just sat there and droned or hummed or something. All day long. They were boring. Sometimes their sounds helped Moxie sleep, though. He kind of droned with them, matching his purring to their tone.

Moxie had two favorites. One was the big-leafed dieffenbachia named Gloria and the other was the crawling philodendron vine, Spanky. They played well together, and if Mox got going real crazy, he'd even jump into their pots. The plants said it tickled, but it usually made a mess and that made Sandra mad. Mox tried real hard not to do that.

But there just wasn't anything else to do in the apartment all day while she was at work. Eat, sleep, and play with the plants.

Moxie listened to Sandra in the kitchen while he looked at the new plant with its fancy foil and purple ribbon, and he nearly died with curiosity. He timed Sandra. She would come out, rub his tummy, tell him to be a good boy, and then she'd be gone for the whole day. He rolled onto his back and put his paws in the air, eyeing the new plant upside down. It was still on *his* windowsill.

"Mox," Sandra said, carrying a box into the living room. "Did you get into the cereal?"

He blinked at her. Cereal?

"No, of course not, what am I thinking?" She rubbed his tummy. "Great Hunters like you don't like bran flakes, do you? Be my Brave Protector and find whoever got into my cereal, okay, sweetie? I'll be home at five-thirty." She scratched his tummy, picked up her purse and keys, and left.

Now.

He flipped over and crouched on the sofa, eyeing the fuzzy plant with the purple flowers. It didn't see him: it was busy basking on *his* windowsill. And singing some foreign song.

He tensed his muscles. He was the Great Cat, the Great Hunter, and this living room was his jungle. His prey was his enemy; it had stolen his territory. His eyes narrowed, his ears lay flat. His pupils dilated, his tail twitched. His rear end began a side-to-side rhythm as his feet got ready. He gauged the distance, knew his approach. Ready, set—

"Don't be silly," the plant said.

He stopped where he was and stood up. "What?"

"You heard me. I said, 'don't be silly.'"

The plant went back to humming that strange song. Not like any song Mox had ever heard before, but like something that maybe he'd dreamed once. A long time ago.

He jumped across to the chair next to the window. "What's so silly?"

"You," the plant said. "You. Pretending you're a beast when you're not."

"I'm a cat. My name's Moxie."

She sneered. "You're a *house* cat. Moxie indeed. 'Moxie' means courage, bravery, nerve. Anyone with that name should have these things."

"I'm a hunter."

"Ha."

Moxie began to wash. He didn't like this new plant.

"So, what are *you?*"

Her leaves raised just a touch, her petals flushed a deeper purple. "I," she said, "am an African violet. You may call me Your Highness."

"Is that your name?"

"That is what you shall call me. I am a Queen."

Moxie began to wash his face. Maybe he should just knock her off the windowsill.

The Queen began to sing.

There was something about the song that made Mox want to relax, close his eyes, and doze. He listened for a while, then sensed her watching him. He turned his back to her and licked his shoulder.

"What is that you're singing?"

"A song of the jungle. It makes you want to go to sleep, doesn't it?"

"How did you know that?"

"Because that's the song in the jungle when the morning comes and it's time for the night hunters to curl up and sleep the day away."

"Have you been to the jungle?" Moxie turned to face her. He forgot all about washing.

"I lived my whole life in the jungle. Until now."

"Wow. Did you see other cats? Like me?"

"My dear. The cats in the jungle are *great* cats, big and lean and strong. They hunt for their food and they live like cats are supposed to live." She paused. "The cats in the jungle have *real* moxie. Not like *some* cats I know."

Moxie jumped down and flicked his tail at her. He sauntered into the kitchen, where his two crystal bowls were filled with fresh food and water. There was a funny smell around his food dishes, but he didn't give it much thought. He had something else on his mind. He lapped water for a minute while he thought about the Queen.

She's not so great. She just sits in a pot.

He picked up a piece of crunch food and munched it, but it would never taste like jungle food again. She'd spoiled that for him.

He sat back and washed his face.

The Queen disturbed him. He'd been happy until she arrived, and now he was dissatisfied with his life. He didn't like her very much, but he had to admit that she was right. Living cooped up in an apartment all the time was no way for a Great Hunter to live. He *had* courage. He *was* brave. Sandra had named him Moxie because she knew those things about him.

He just didn't have any way to prove it to that stupid jungle plant.

He looked at the Queen out of the corner of his eye as she radiated in the early morning sunlight. *I'm going to knock her down*, he thought. He jumped onto the couch, then onto the chair next to her window, then leaped gently to her side.

"I'm going to knock you down," he said.

"Why, because I told you the truth?"

"I don't like it."

"The truth? My boy, the truth is good. You should always tell the truth. And believe the truth."

"You made me wonder about things."

"Ah, well. Wonder is good, too."

"How?"

"Because when you wonder, you awaken. You want to discover things."

"I know everything already. In the apartment, I mean."

"Well, then, I think it's time to broaden your horizons."

"What do you mean?"

"Go outside."

"Outside!" Mox looked through the window at the scene he knew perfectly. He'd gazed through that window every day all day for his entire life, yet he'd never thought of going out there. How would he get out there? How would he get back? What would he do?

Then the Queen began to sing a different song. She sang softly at first, and a fire began to rise within him. He felt the stripes on his sides and his forehead begin to glow. He felt the power again, the real instincts of a Great Cat.

He closed his eyes and with the Queen's song in his head, he felt himself outside for the first time.

Outside was loud. And big. From his windowsill, everything looked small, but out here, it wasn't.

He saw the big tree that he could see from his window. It was huge. It reached all the way to the sky. He bunched his muscles and bounded toward it. His running rhythm was free and easy; he'd never known such pleasure as his muscles moved smoothly and he ran like the wind.

The tree grew larger as he approached it. Without thinking, he jumped at it and ran straight up the trunk. He clung to it with all his claws out, then hitched up a couple more inches until he reached a branch. He climbed out on the branch and rested. He licked his paws.

Look at me, he said to himself. *I'm sitting in a tree!*

He saw a brown leaf and made it into—a bird! He stalked it, pounced on it, and tore it to shreds. He climbed up to the next branch and found a little stick, tied to the tree by an old spider web. He made it into—a mouse! He chased it, caught it, wrestled it from its clinging trap, and dropped it below. He was hunting!

A new courage and a new feeling came through him. He *was* a real cat. He *could* hunt. He could do *anything*. Climb a tree. Run across a parking lot. He could do anything.

Then the Queen's song changed and Moxie blinked open his eyes.

That had been a dream? It all seemed so real...

The Queen wouldn't talk after that; she just kept humming to herself. Moxie went back to the bedroom and napped and dreamed normal half-awake cat dreams, but he couldn't forget the experience he'd had of being outside his window.

The next morning, Moxie yawned and stretched, listening for Sandra to begin puttering around in the kitchen. He waited to hear the rustle of his kitty food bag, but he didn't hear it. He wondered what was taking her so long.

He jumped off the bed, gave a mighty stretch, felt his body wake up from his long sleep, and went to see what Sandra was doing.

She wasn't even in the kitchen. She was in the living room, watering can in hand, looking at all the plants with a dark expression on her face. He could smell something, that same something he smelled the morning before, but he didn't know what it was.

"Moxie, come here. Look at this."

He jumped up onto the couch to see what she was looking at. Two of the big squatty plants had holes in them; big chunks were missing out of their sides.

"And this." She picked him up and carried him to the other side of the room, where Spanky was whining, the end leaves of his vine clipped right off and lying on the floor. Magnolia's leaves were strewn all about her pot, and scrape marks on her trunk showed stark white wood beneath. Even Lucas and Joseph were oozing white blood from tears in their stems.

"And this. Look at *this*, Mox."

The Queen. Several of her fuzzy leaves had been shredded, and her purple flowers lay torn and blackening on the windowsill around her pot.

"Did *you* do this, Mox?"

Moxie's heart stuck in his throat. How could Sandra imagine he had done these terrible things to his friends? He smelled her anger, smelled her disappointment, and he couldn't stand it. He struggled in her arms until she dropped him.

"Bad cat," she said, and he wanted to die.

He hid under the end table until she was finished watering. She put food in one bowl and filled the other with fresh water, but he was too ashamed to face her. Maybe he had done the terrible things and didn't remember. Who else could have?

Sandra finished cleaning up the plants, then left without a good-bye, without a belly scratch, without their usual playtime. Moxie had never felt so empty. He licked his shoulders and listened to the plants as they moaned to themselves.

The poor Queen. *I hope* she *doesn't think I did it,* he thought. He came out from under the end table and saw her sitting in the window, her silhouette wilted and torn. He jumped lightly onto the sill and touched the edge of her pot with his paw.

"Don't touch me!"

He jerked back.

"You stupid!"

"What did I do?"

"What did you do? It's what you *didn't* do! Look at us! Torn limb from limb. It was a massacre in here last night, and you slept peacefully through it all, on Sandra's nice soft bed."

"What happened?"

"*What happened?* Smell my leaves."

Moxie took a few tentative sniffs. It was the same odor. Something he had never smelled before, but it made the fur rise on his back. "What is that?"

"Rat, Moxie, *rat.*"

Moxie was horrified, even though he wasn't sure what a rat was.

"How did a rat get in here?"

"Through the kitchen cabinet."

"I have to tell Sandra that it's not my fault."

"Rats always let others take the blame for what they do. That's why they're rats. A cat with any moxie at all will smell the rat, hunt it down, and kill it. But you... Some cat *you* are. All *you* can think to do is to tell Sandra that it's not *your* fault. Well, what about us? Are you going to let him come in here tonight and finish eating us?"

Moxie felt bad, but he didn't know what to do. He didn't want the rat to eat the plants, but he certainly didn't want to hunt and kill it. Hunting and killing was fun, like when he made a piece of paper into a leaf, or a leaf into a bird, but to hunt a real rat... He jumped onto the coffee table and began to wash.

"In the jungle," the Queen said, "there is balance. Everybody and everything has a purpose. Even plants, after they are dead, become good soil for the next generation. Nothing is wasted. And it's everybody's responsibility to do his job so that everything stays in balance."

Moxie understood this. The Queen made so much sense. He began to purr as he listened to her soft voice.

"Sometimes the jungle gets out of balance, but only for a little while, because there is always something there to fix it. There are rats in the jungle, Mox, but there are also cats. Right now, this apartment is out of balance. We can't fix the hole in the cabinet, so you have to kill the rat. You're the cat."

Moxie stopped purring and looked around at his friends. Gloria rustled her leaves. Magnolia let loose a new shower of leaves to fall on the carpeting. Spanky shook his vine, and Wakefield-Smith trembled. The cacti moaned. Lucas and Joseph conferred quietly among themselves.

"I can't," Moxie said.

"Of course you can. If you are a Great Hunter, you can. Just follow your natural instincts. Let your real moxie come out."

Moxie jumped down and went into the bedroom. He was afraid he didn't *have* any real moxie. Sure, he could imagine he was outside in a tree when the Queen sang to him, but his friends were counting on him to save them. It was a big responsibility. Too big.

He stayed in the bedroom until Sandra came home. He watched her brush her hair and put on her nightie. When she snuggled down under the covers, he wanted to curl up in her hair the way he used to do when he was a kitten, but she was still mad at him, so he didn't dare.

The nighttime sounds of the apartment were familiar, and Mox kept his ears open, listening to all the quiet whisperings of the plants, even though he slept. He slept through the refrigerator sounds and the clock chimes, but when he heard the crunch of his cat food in the middle of the dark, dark night, he came wide awake.

In one moment, his eyes were open, his head was up, his ears were pointed toward the kitchen, and the gray fur stood up along his spine. Carefully, so as not to wake Sandra, he got up, a growl low in his throat, and he jumped off the bed.

He heard tiny little crunches, and as he peeked around the corner, he saw a dark shape hunched over his crystal bowl.

"Hey," Moxie said, and the rat's head snapped up and looked at him with beady black eyes. The rat's nose began to twitch fine little whiskers. A crumb of cat food hung on his chin. Long yellowed front teeth stuck out of his mouth.

"Cat, eh?" the rat said. "Cat. Hmmm. Cat."

"You're eating my food," Moxie said. "Who are you, anyway?" The rat backed away from the bowl, and keeping his eyes on Moxie, ran lightly around the kitchen floor, long, skinny, snakelike tail following him. Now Moxie could identify the smell, and his fur stood up even higher.

Moxie watched the rat run on his tiny feet, thinking it was a pretty funny-looking creature, when the plants began to wail.

The rat scurried next to the wall, from the kitchen to the living room, and quickly climbed up the couch and ran lightly along the cactus shelf.

"Hey," Moxie said. "What are you doing?"

"Snack," the rat said.

Magnolia dropped a whole shower of leaves.

"No, those are my friends. You can't eat my friends."

"Snack, snack," the rat said, and keeping his eyes on Moxie, began to paw at the dirt in a cactus pot.

"No." Moxie crossed the living room and jumped up onto the couch. "No. Now you get down from there."

The rat bit into the cactus, sinking his long front teeth deep into the tender plant. Mox heard the high-pitched whine of the cactus.

"Stop that!"

"Yum," said the rat as he took another bite. Then his furry little body hustled along the ledge toward the windowsill, long tail slithering along behind him.

I don't like this, Moxie thought as he watched the rat jump up onto the windowsill. "That's enough," he said. "I want you to leave."

"Snack," the rat said, looking directly at him.

"She's not a snack, she's a Queen. Her name is Your Highness."

The rat looked at the fragile, trembling plant with the regal purple ribbon tied around her tin-foiled pot and said, "Yum."

"No!" Moxie yelled, but the rat darted in and grabbed a mouthful of fuzzy leaf, tearing it.

The Queen screamed once and fainted.

"I hate you," Moxie said, and then, in the back of his mind, he heard the Queen's music. He heard it loud and strong and it reminded him of his true nature, it reminded him of Fearless Hunter, of Great Cat. He remembered being "outside" the day before, and he knew he could do *anything*. He leaped to the sill.

The rat reared up on his big hind legs, eyes shining with menace, long yellow front teeth gleaming with nastiness. Mox landed on top of him, and they both juggled for balance along the narrow sill. The rat's heavy rear swung around and knocked the Queen down, but Moxie barely noticed. He grabbed the rat by the back of the neck just as the rat sank his ugly teeth into Moxie's leg, then they both fell to the floor, Mox hitting his chin hard.

He heard the tiniest crunch as they landed, not any louder than the rat munching his kitty food, and the rat went limp.

Mox backed away, blood running down his leg, and he said, "Rat? Rat?" Mox poked him once with his paw, but the rat didn't move.

Then he saw the Queen. Her ribboned planter had rolled away from her, leaving her pot-shaped moss and tender white roots showing, her shredded leaves limp, her beautiful blossoms scattered about her.

"Your Highness? Your Highness?" There was no answer.

There was only one thing to do. Moxie ran into the bedroom and jumped up onto Sandra's bed.

"Meow," he said, and Sandra's sleepy hand found his head and petted him. *"Meow,"* he said louder, and pushed his cold nose into her eyelid.

"Not now, Mox," she said, and scratched behind his ears.

Moxie backed off, just out of reach, sat down, and began to yowl. He yowled in fear and worry for the Queen, and he yowled because he was filled with so many feelings that his stomach hurt and he didn't know what else to do.

Sandra sat up and turned on the light. "What's the matter? Oh, Mox, you're bleeding."

Mox jumped down and Sandra followed. He stood over the Queen, and when Sandra turned on the light, she gasped. "Oh, my violet!" and hurried to put the Queen right. Sandra settled the Queen gently back into her pot and took her into the kitchen.

Moxie went to sit next to the rat. Sandra should help it next.

A few minutes later, she came out. "Now," she said. "Let's look at your leg."

Moxie had even forgotten that he had been bitten.

"Oh!" she said, her hands flying to her mouth. "You killed a rat! Oh, a *big* rat! Oh, Moxie, it was a rat that was hurting the plants and I blamed you." She picked him up and cuddled him the way she always did, the way he loved the best. "I'm sure it was that old rat that got into my cereal, too," she said, stroking his fur. He began to purr. "I'm sorry, sweetie."

He held real still while she looked at his leg. She wiped the blood away and kissed him between the ears. The bite wasn't bad; he'd lick it better in no time.

Sandra picked the rat up by his snaky tail and put him into a garbage sack and down the hallway chute. Then she took Moxie back to bed, where they cuddled for the rest of the night.

In the morning, when she called him her Brave Hunter, he knew she meant it. And when the Queen woke up, he was by her side to comfort her, and she began to heal right away, too.

A workman came and fixed the hole in the kitchen cabinet,

and Moxie felt that balance was back in the apartment.

Soon the Queen was well enough to go back to the windowsill, and Moxie sat by her side with pride. They sat there every day. They talked and laughed with the others; he purred while she sang. And he always called her "Your Highness," and she always called him "Mr. Moxie."

There was plenty of room on the windowsill, he discovered, for friends.

How we wrote our story...

Suzanne was given the job of naming the boy in our story. I decided Mandel could be shortened to Manny. Mandel sounded like a person who should be as smart as Einstein, or maybe play the concert piano. I didn't see Manny playing a piano.

We decided together that the story would be about a boy who tells stories that sometimes get him into trouble. He was a boy with a big imagination. It was my idea that Manny turn out to be a real hero because I like heroes, and I liked Manny.

Suzanne and I collaborated this way: I typed the story on my computer and then she would read over the draft and make changes. At one point I had Manny saying that Mr. Banner's back was "as stiff as a skateboard." Suzanne let me know that a skateboard isn't all that stiff. It has to bend and give to be a very good skateboard.

Because our story ran long, I did the necessary cutting. Suzanne knew what details could be left out.

We didn't argue or fight over Manny's story, not even a little. Some collaborators might argue and have artistic differences, but Suzanne is like Manny—she's always known better than to argue with Mom.

Billie Sue Mosiman   *Suzanne Mosiman Garcia*

THE REAL-LIFE ADVENTURES OF MANNY FITZ

BY BILLIE SUE MOSIMAN
AND SUZANNE MOSIMAN GARCIA

Mandel stared at the Saint Ecstasy cake on the sideboard near the table, his mouth watering. "I can't have just *one* piece? Or a bite? Not even a bite?"

"If you tell a story, then you go without dessert. You know the rules, Mandel."

But Saint Ecstasy cake was his favorite. Little bits of mandarin oranges in the cake, whipped cream with crushed pineapple in the topping.

"But, Mom, I didn't…"

She raised her fork, tines pointing to the ceiling, a warning to hush. "I do not believe Mrs. Forsythe keeps a boa constrictor in her apartment. Mandel, you've got to stop this storytelling. Next time punishment will be more than missing dessert."

Mandel scowled silently at his plate. Okay, it wasn't a boa. It was a green plastic garter snake that Mrs. Forsythe's grandson left behind after his visit on Sunday. But was that interesting, a plastic snake? He couldn't help it if his stories had a way of getting…bigger.

He eyed the cake one last time, sighed noisily so his mother would be sure to hear him, and excused himself from the table.

"Don't wander far."

He wouldn't. The apartment house his mother owned and managed was his castle. The steps substituted for a throne. The tenants were, depending on his mood, his servants, his knights in armor, his closest cohorts in a secret royal intrigue.

Sometimes the house was a fort and he was the cavalry Captain. At other times, the house was a giant sailing ship on pirate-infested seas.

Not that he wouldn't have enjoyed playing away from the house on the street with the other kids once in a while, but they wouldn't have him. Called him Lie-Face, Big Liar, and Mouth. Was it his fault Joey was really in the park running after a pretty older girl named Emily when Joey's mom asked Mandel where her son was? Oh, man, Joey never forgave him for that.

The guys stopped picking Mandel for their side in games or inviting him anywhere. Actually, they just stopped speaking to him altogether.

It didn't matter. He didn't need them. He didn't need anyone to have fun.

He sat on the first riser of the steps waiting for Peggy Duberry to come home from work.

Peggy looked like Madonna's little sister. She always said "Hello, what did you do today?"

Most grownups had closed-up faces, like figures in comic books, but not Peggy.

The front door opened and Peggy swept into the vestibule, wind chasing at her back.

Mandel breathed deeply the scent of the hot street that came in on the wind. Soft sunny asphalt, car exhaust, weenie and sauerkraut smells from Karmouchi's vendor cart parked on the corner.

"Hello, Manny, how are you today?" She was the only tenant who called him Manny. She was the only person in the whole world who called him Manny. He liked it so much that next year when school started, he'd tell everyone that was his name.

"I'm okay. How was work?"

"Oh, work was fine." She swung her hair back from her shoulders. It was white hair, bleached, his mother said. Mandel thought it was like angel hair you put around the tree at Christmastime and hoped Peggy wouldn't ever stop bleaching it. She confided one day that she'd had *purple* hair before moving to the apartment house. Purple—wow. He would give anything to have seen that.

"Gotta run, Manny. Need a shower."

He scooted to one side of the riser so she could pass. He always heard the pipes in the walls gurgling minutes after she got into her apartment on the second floor.

Thinking about how he'd figured out Peggy's routine, he was struck with a grand thought. Maybe he'd start a detective agency this week. He could pretend to be Humphrey Bogart and talk from the side of his mouth.

Might as well start now. "We got a new person in 3B. I think he's a spy for...for...the Chinese."

Peggy had started up the stairs, but she paused. "There's a new tenant? In 3B?"

"Yeah, he's a spy, all right. He wears wrinkled suits and brown shoes. Only spies wear brown shoes."

Peggy smiled. Her teeth were little and square like pegs on the board puzzle he kept in his room. "Why do you think he's a spy?"

Mandel thought real hard. "He…well, he's got a telescope."

"Hmmm…okay, you keep an eye on things, Manny. You never know when events might require investigation."

He sat chewing his lower lip. The day the guy, Mr. Banner, moved in, Mandel watched but stayed out of the way. When he saw the strange carrying case and couldn't make out what might be in it, he inquired, "What's that?"

Mr. Banner stopped and stared at him. "It's a telescope. Do you live here?"

"I'm Mandel Fitz. My mom's the landlady."

"I study the stars," Mr. Banner offered. "It's a hobby."

"Can't see many stars from here," Mandel said. "Too many tall buildings."

"Oh, you'd be surprised," Mr. Banner said, leaving abruptly.

So Mr. Banner *could* be a spy. Spies used telescopes. They were creepy, sneaky people, spies. You couldn't trust them to tell the truth.

Mandel was lining up three toy soldiers on the rubber floor runner, about to shoot them dead with a toy pistol, when Mrs. Forsythe came out of her door and nearly plopped over his legs. She stumbled, whacking his calves good with her clod-hopper old-lady shoes. "Ow!"

"Well, young man, if you wouldn't play in front of my door, I wouldn't run into you."

"Yes, ma'am."

She had a string bag dangling from one arm and her black patent purse from the other.

"I think Peggy said they had peaches big as watermelons down at the Super Bargain."

Mrs. Forsythe said without turning around, "Peaches don't grow as big as watermelons, Mandel."

She was out the door, the vestibule invaded with summer sunshine and heat for a moment. Maybe he should have said peaches as big as *grapefruit*. Mrs. Forsythe would have believed that, he bet.

Charlie Masters came running down the stairs full tilt, books in his hands. He took accounting classes.

"Mrs. Forsythe keeps a boa constrictor," Mandel said, hoping to slow him down.

Charlie pounded to the bottom of the steps and shifted his books onto one hip. "Your mother allow that?"

Mandel shrugged. "She don't know about it."

"A boa? You mean an anaconda, like from the jungle? In her apartment?" He glanced fearfully at Mrs. Forsythe's door.

"It's not a big boa. It's a baby. Only six feet long."

"Oh, man."

"Maybe it's just four feet. I didn't see it up close."

"Well, I hope you tell your mother right away. No pets allowed, that's what the lease papers say. Next we'll have ferrets and potbelly pigs and dogs and cats—oh, man, cats. I'm allergic to cats."

"I'll tell her. She'll ask Mrs. Forsythe to take it to the zoo."

"I should hope so." He raced for the door and swooped out like a crane, all skinny legs and arms.

Mr. Banner came in at three o'clock. Mandel had set up a cardboard desk against the wall, waiting for clients. "Want me to track down someone for you, Mr. Banner?"

The man frowned, and Mandel saw that his eyes were almost black. Not brown at all, as he had thought. Black, like soot inside a dirty fireplace.

"Not today," he said.

"Where do you work?" Mandel asked.

"I beg your pardon?"

"It's early. No one comes home this early. You must have a good job."

"I'm sorry…what's your name?"

"Manny."

"I'm sorry, Manny, but I don't really have time to chat. I've got some work to do and then an appointment."

Mandel watched him move up the stairs, his back as stiff as a board. Chat? He didn't have time to *chat?* Well, that was a foreign-sounding thing to say to a kid. Mandel would investigate his lease for sounding like an Englishman.

The next day, Peggy Duberry hired Manny to investigate.

Well, she didn't hire him to investigate Mr. Banner specifically, but she had put down a dollar bill on Mandel's collapsible cardboard desk in the corner of the foyer and told him it was payment for his time and trouble. "I hear noise at night," she said. "It's probably squirrels running up the tree outside my window. They could be getting into the attic eaves and making nests."

He had the apartment house to himself. His mother was downstairs mopping the kitchen, and the other tenants were all gone for the day. Even Mrs. Forsythe was gone. She'd left earlier with her daughter-in-law to spend two days at her son's house baby-sitting their new baby.

He crept up the stairs, his plastic pistol drawn for protection. He listened at each of the tenant's doors carefully before proceeding to the next one. He knew they were gone, but a good private eye had to be certain.

When he got to 3B, he approached the door on tiptoe. He noticed 3B was right above Peggy's apartment and decided the noises she'd heard might have come from inside.

What kind of noise could Mr. Banner be making that sounded like a bunch of squirrels scratching around?

Mandel rushed down the stairs again, intent on getting the keys. His mother didn't know, of course, that he sneaked the keys and checked out the new people whenever they moved in. If she knew, he'd be grounded for weeks. Holy cripes, she could never know half the things he got into.

It wasn't as if he did any harm, he told himself, sneaking quietly through his own apartment to his mother's bedroom and the extra key drawer. He never *touched* anything in other people's apartments. He wasn't a *burglar*.

He found the key marked with orange tape with 3B written in indelible ink on it and stuffed it into his pocket.

He left the apartment again without his mother noticing he'd ever entered. He hurried up the stairs to the third floor, got the passkey in the lock, and looked over his shoulder to make sure he was still alone.

It was kind of scary being an investigator. No wonder Bogey always carried some kind of weapon. You could run into some sticky situations.

He was inside, the door closed at his back. He held his breath, waiting for his heart to slow down. It felt as if a fast car had gotten into his chest and was revving the engines for a drag race.

His vision adjusted to the interior shadows. The window blinds were closed so that ribbons of pale sunlight marched across the carpet and up the wall.

He took two steps and stopped, looking around. Mr. Banner kept the place spotless. Clean as a whistle.

Nothing on the tables or the counter that separated the living area from the kitchen. No magazines or books or papers anywhere.

Maybe Mr. Banner didn't read. Not *anything*. It looked as if no one even lived here. There were no photographs or knick-knacks or ashtrays. No mail, no candy jars, nothing, nothing, nothing. It was as empty as it had been before Mr. Banner moved in.

Mandel went to the bathroom and peeked inside. Even the

sink gleamed, a pale pearl against the wall. Towels were folded neatly and stacked on the toilet lid.

He left, tiptoeing across the frayed carpet to the bedroom door. It was closed. He slid his palm onto his shirt front to wipe away sweat before he took the doorknob into his hand. He looked inside the room and saw the bed was made, which didn't surprise him, but then he saw the telescope set up at the window opposite the bed. He went to it and wondered if Mr. Banner did much stargazing.

He put his hands behind his back so he wouldn't touch the telescope. Then he leaned forward and went up onto tiptoes to peer through the lens. Clear as day, he saw one wide window in the apartment building across the street. A man was there. He wore a suit and held a phone to his ear as he walked past the window and back again.

Frowning, Mandel dropped down to flat feet. Was Mr. Banner a Peeping Tom, looking in people's windows? That wasn't legal, was it?

Mandel shivered. *He might come in*, he thought. *He might find you here.*

Better get out.

Mandel was about to scurry away when he saw that the closet door next to the bed was open. Something inside drew his attention—a tall black case. Not the same one Mr. Banner carried the telescope in.

Mandel gently removed the black case, finding it heavy. He laid it on the floor and squatted, opening the snaps that kept it closed. He lifted the lid.

For some time he didn't know what he was looking at. That's because it was all in pieces. Packed into black foam-filled indentations in the case. A polished wood stock. A black barrel. A fancy telescopic lens attachment.

It was a very big gun. A big, bad, really scary gun.

Mandel quickly shut the lid, and now his hands were trembling. He glanced back over his shoulder at the window and the big telescope.

Mr. Banner was going to kill someone. That's all this could mean.

He might kill the man across the street.

The latches on the gun case clicked shut with a finality that made Mandel flinch. He set it into place where he had found it.

Downstairs he burst into his own apartment calling, "Mom! Mom!"

She came from the kitchen, her hands folded into a kitchen towel. "What is it? Why are you shouting?"

He drew in his breath and was about to say, "Mr. Banner's going to kill someone, he has a gun, and he's been watching the guy across the street," when the gravity of what he had done hit home. His mother didn't know he had been taking the keys and intruding on the tenants' apartments. She'd know now. She'd punish him severely. Worse, she'd be disappointed in him.

"Uh...uh..."

"Well, what is it? You look as if you saw a ghost."

Not yet, he thought.

"I...uh...Mr. Banner..."

"What about Mr. Banner?"

"Well, Mom, he's…"

"What? He's what?"

"He's a spy!" Oh, now, he didn't mean to say that at all. It just popped out of his mouth and he couldn't get it back.

She stopped drying her hands. "Mr. Banner is not a spy. I think you'll do the supper dishes tonight."

"Okay, Mom, he's not a spy, but he's a bad man. I swear it. He's got a telescope and he watches this guy across the street with it and in his closet…"

"I will not listen to any more of your lies. This is it, Mandel." She paused, staring at him curiously now. "How do you know he watches someone with a telescope? Did he tell you?"

"No, but I saw…"

A knock sounded at the door.

Mr. Banner stood in the doorway. Mandel felt his heart lurch. What if he'd come home just minutes earlier and found Mandel poking around in his apartment? He might have killed him or something. Tied him up and put him in the closet to starve. Kidnapped him and taken him out to New Jersey.

"Mrs. Fitz, I wanted to let you know that I'll be leaving for a few days. I have to fly to the West Coast, family business. If you don't see me around, that's why."

"All right, Mr. Banner. Thank you for letting me know. I'd worry, otherwise." As soon as she shut the door, Mandel scooted past her, opened the door again, and ran into the foyer.

"Mandel, I think we have something we weren't through discussing!"

Mandel was already at the door and outside, leaping down the steps to the sidewalk.

Mr. Banner was going to his apartment. He was going away somewhere soon. Something wasn't right.

He looked up at the front of the red-brick apartment house to 3B's window. He looked over across the street at the window he had seen in the telescope. It, too, was on the third floor. He couldn't see if the man with the telephone was there or not. Sunlight filled the rectangular pane of glass, plating it gold.

He knew what he must do. Tell the man across the street. Now, this instant.

He heard his mother calling his name, but he couldn't wait. He sprinted across the street and ran into the apartment building.

The elevator was carpeted and so quiet that he heard himself whispering, "Hurry, hurry." As soon as the doors slid apart on the third floor, he ran out, then he stopped. Which of these apartments faced his own across the street?

He tried hard to imagine the outside of the building and the placement of the windows. He decided it was the middle apartment. He knocked and kept knocking, *bap, bap, bap.* The man with the telephone suddenly stood there, the electronic phone in his fist. "What do you want?"

It all tumbled out. "There's a man across the street in apartment 3B who has a telescope. It looks right into your window and he's got a gun case in the closet and he just said he's going away for a while, but he might take out the gun, because he's been watching you, and he might..."

"Whoa, hold on there, pardner. What is it you're rattling on about? Someone across the street and he's been watching my window?"

Mandel swallowed, out of breath, and nodded vigorously.

"I'll call you back, Jerry," the man said into the receiver. He clicked the OFF button and strode across the room. Mandel followed him in. He saw the man going to the wide window.

"Hey, don't go over..."

As the man turned back toward Mandel, there was a breaking sound. Then came a loud thump in the wall behind Mandel, followed by the falling of plaster chips. A hole appeared in the window and around it radiated rays as if from a star. Mandel fell to the floor, his legs giving way beneath him. He started crying, blubbering like a baby, and hating that, really hating it. He crawled across the carpet to the sofa, and around it. He saw the man lying on the carpet, groaning.

"Did he hit you? Are you shot?"

The man's eyes were closed and he rocked from side to side, groaning. Mandel found the dropped telephone and grabbed it. He glanced fearfully at the window ledge, glad the gunman across the street couldn't see them down here.

He called 911 and reported what had happened. Then he called his mom and in a breathless voice told her. Once he'd done that, he felt all over the man on the floor, looking for a wound. He found a wet spot on the man's suit near the shoulder blade. He said, still crying and not able to stop, "You'll be all right, you'll be okay, mister, they'll send someone soon to help us."

☠ ☠ ☠

Mrs. Fitz was the first to reach her son and the stranger. She grabbed two mauve throw pillows from the sofa and placed one on each side of the bleeding man's shoulder blade.

Next came the paramedics, who brought in a stretcher, lifted up the stranger, and toted him out. Before they were out the door, two police officers and a man in a blue suit entered the apartment. Mandel could hear the wail of sirens and the sound of tires screeching to a stop out on the street below.

The detective—a real one, Mandel realized—began his questions. Mandel answered them as best he could, and the two policemen were sent across the street to 3B.

"Well, son, you just saved a man's life. I think the department might give you a citation of bravery for this. Maybe the mayor will even want to meet you."

Mandel didn't care about that. He was just glad it was over.

On the way across the street with the detective, Mandel said, "Did they catch him?" Mandel wasn't going inside until he knew.

"They secured your apartment building and he wasn't there, so they went on foot into the neighborhood. Caught him red-handed with the gun case four blocks from here."

The detective looked down at Mandel. "How did you know he had a gun and he planned to do this?"

Mandel saw they were leading Mr. Banner down the sidewalk, his hands cuffed behind him.

"Well, I'm a private investigator," Mandel said. "And I snitched the extra key to his apartment from my mom's drawer where she keeps them. I thought I'd have a little look around…"

He had thought his mother had already entered the house, but she must have been standing right behind Mandel and the detective because now she spoke up. "Mandel! You've been taking my keys and going into the tenants' apartments? Why I ought to—"

The detective turned and said quietly, "Perhaps the boy should be forgiven this time, Mrs. Fitz. After all, if he hadn't sneaked around, he might not have saved someone's life today."

"Well, I suppose…"

Mandel watched his mother closely to be sure she was convinced. He didn't want to have to stay inside their apartment for the next two million summer vacations without television privileges.

After she had left them to answer another policeman's questions, Mandel turned to the detective and put out his hand. "Thanks," he said, feeling relieved. "My mom would have toasted me if you hadn't helped out."

"No problem." He took Mandel's hand and smiled. "You're a good kid, don't forget that."

Mandel felt a blush creep into his cheeks. To combat it, he said, "Have you ever seen a boa constrictor?"

The detective shook his head. "Don't believe I have."

"Well, one of our tenants, a certain Mrs. Forsythe—she's in 1B on the first floor—keeps a great big boa constrictor in her apartment. She probably feeds it stray cats. She always says she doesn't like cats," said Mandel.

"Is that right?"

Mandel smiled and straightened his shoulders. "Well, maybe it's not a boa. Maybe I saw it in the shadows or something. It could have been just a garter snake."

"Yeah?"

"Might even have been a plastic one."

"Umm-hmm."

"Well, anyway, if you ever need help on a case, I have my office inside," Mandel said, starting up the steps. "I don't charge a whole lot either."

He skipped to the top step and disappeared into the darkness.

Peggy Duberry would be home soon and he needed to let her know how well he had earned the dollar she gave him. Charlie Masters would come in, loaded down with books, and he'd be interested to know what an exciting day he had missed. Mrs. Forsythe would be back in two days. She'd just love to know she could count on Mandel to keep the apartment house safe.

And maybe Mom would make a Saint Ecstasy cake to celebrate. She might even let him have two slices if he remembered to tell her about the squirrel nests that were probably filling up the back eaves of the house.

Or were those dragon lairs? Little dragons. Peggy may have thought they were squirrels because she didn't look close. But they were dragons, all right, maybe from Mars, where the Martians grew them small to invade Earth. It was the beginning of the end for mankind…

He'd have to decide all the details and get the story perfect—just perfect—before he tried it out on her.

ABOUT THE GREAT WRITERS

MAX ALLAN COLLINS is a two-time winner of the Private Eye Writers of America Shamus Award for his popular Nathan Heller novels. He has received an unprecedented six nominations for that award. He lives in Muscatine, Iowa, with his wife, the writer Barbara Collins, and their son, Nathan.

BARBARA D'AMATO, the 1995 president of Sisters in Crime International, was awarded both the Anthony and the Agatha awards for her mystery *The Doctor, the Murder, the Mystery*. Her series about Chicago freelance reporter Cat Marsala includes the books *Hardball*, *Hard Tack*, *Hard Luck*, *Hard Women*, *Hard Case*, and *Hard Christmas*. She lives in Illinois.

CAROLE NELSON DOUGLAS was an award-winning journalist before becoming a novelist. She is a writer of many different genres, including fantasy and science fiction. In the mystery field, she has created two popular series. *Good Night, Mr. Holmes* launched the adventures of Irene Adler, the only woman to outwit Sherlock Holmes. It was a *New York Times* Notable Book as well as a winner of an American Mystery Award. Ms. Douglas's Midnight Louie mystery series stars the very same feline supersleuth found in her story for this collection. Ms. Douglas lives in Fort Worth, Texas, with her husband, six cats, and a species-confused dog.

ELIZABETH ENGSTROM has twice been nominated for the Horror Writers Association Bram Stoker Award. Her books cross genres from mystery to suspense and horror. Her titles include *Lizard Wine* and *Lizzie Borden*, a fictionalized account of the infamous day in 1892 that gave America one of its most notorious crime stories. When not on the road leading seminars or speaking at conferences, Ms. Engstrom makes her home in Oregon.

ED GORMAN has sold more than three million copies of his books worldwide. England's *Million* magazine called him "one of the world's great storytellers," while the *San Francisco Examiner* noted that "Gorman has a wonderful writing style that allows him to say things of substance in an entertaining way." His work has been nominated for both the Edgar Allan Poe Award (the Edgar) and the Anthony Award, and he has won the Shamus. He lives in Iowa with his wife, Carol, who is also a writer.

WENDY HORNSBY is the author of six mystery novels and many short stories, including "Nine Sons," for which she won an Edgar Award. Her work has also received the American Mystery Award and an Anthony nomination. *Publishers Weekly* declared her latest book, *77th Street Requiem,* "one of the most gripping, compelling mysteries of the year." Ms. Hornsby holds graduate degrees in ancient and medieval history and teaches history at the college level. She lives in Southern California with her son, Chris. Her daughter, Alyson, who is herself a published writer, is a student at American University in Washington, D.C.

STUART KAMINSKY is the author of many mystery novels. His Inspector Porfiry Rostnikov series, set in contemporary Russia, includes *A Cold Red Sunrise,* which won the Edgar Award for Best Mystery. He is also the author of the Abe Lieberman mysteries, which focus on a Chicago policeman, and the Toby Peters mysteries, which follow the comic adventures of a private detective in 1940s Hollywood. Mr. Kaminsky, a native of Chicago, presently resides with his family in Sarasota, Florida.

JONATHAN KELLERMAN is a former child psychologist and the author of eleven successive *New York Times* best-selling novels, including *When the Bough Breaks, Blood Test, Over the Edge, Silent Partner, Time Bomb, Private Eyes, Devil's Waltz, Bad Love, Self-Defense,* and *The Web.* Dr. Kellerman's books have won the Edgar, the Anthony, and the Samuel Goldwyn awards. He is also the author of two books on psychology and two children's books, *Daddy, Daddy, Can You Touch the Sky?* and *Jonathan Kellerman's ABC of Weird Creatures.* He is the proud father of four very talented children, including Ilana, with whom he writes in this collection. He is married to the novelist Faye Kellerman and resides in California.

SHARYN McCRUMB is the author of fourteen novels, including the highly acclaimed Ballad Books series, which consists of *If Ever I Return, Pretty Peggy-O, The Hangman's Beautiful Daughter,* and *She Walks These Hills,* all of which were named *New York Times* Notable Books. Ms. McCrumb has won the McCavity Award and the Agatha Award, and has been nominated for the Weatherford, Nero, and Anthony awards. A native of North Carolina, she now lives in the Virginia Blue Ridge with her husband, David, an environmental engineer, and their children, Spencer and Laura.

BILLIE SUE MOSIMAN is the Edgar-nominated author of seven novels of suspense and more than eighty-five short stories. Her latest novels are *Widow* and *Stiletto*. Ms. Mosiman collaborates in this collection with Suzanne Mosiman Garcia, her eldest daughter and "best good friend." Billie Sue Mosiman lives in Texas.

JOAN LOWERY NIXON has authored over one hundred books for young people. She is a multiple winner of the Edgar Award for Best Juvenile Fiction and has won many Children's Choice Awards. Her series for children include the Orphan Train Adventures and the mystery series the Casebusters. She lives with her husband in Houston, Texas.

SCOTT TUROW is an attorney and an author. His first book, *One L*, about his experience as a first-year student at Harvard Law School, was published in 1977. Ten years later, he achieved a lifelong ambition with the publication of his first novel, *Presumed Innocent*, followed by *Burden of Proof* and *Pleading Guilty*. Mr. Turow's books have won a number of literary awards. They have been translated into more than twenty languages, and have sold nearly twenty million copies worldwide. Scott Turow continues to practice law as a partner in the Chicago office of Sonnenschein, Carlin, Nath & Rosenthal.

PATRICIA WALLACE is the author of the Sydney Bryant mystery series, the fourth book of which, *Deadly Devotion*, was nominated for a Shamus Award for Best PI Paperback. (Sydney herself makes an appearance as a young girl in Ms. Wallace's story for this collection.) Ms. Wallace is also the author of eleven horror novels and the suspense thriller *Dark Intent*. She has degrees in film and police science, and she resides in Nevada with her husband.

ABOUT THE EDITORS

MARTIN H. GREENBERG is the foremost anthologist in the world, with hundreds of collections to his credit. His projects for children include the Newbery Series, featuring stories by authors who have won the Newbery Medal.

JILL M. MORGAN is the author of adult, young-adult, and middle-grade novels in a variety of genres, including mystery.

ROBERT WEINBERG has edited nearly one hundred anthologies. An author himself, he lectures widely on the subject of genre fiction.

ABOUT THE ILLUSTRATOR

GAHAN WILSON has been praised as a national treasure. Since the 1950s, he has amused children and adults alike with his weirdly funny creatures, which have appeared in books and magazines as diverse as *The New Yorker*, *Omni*, and *National Lampoon*.

Sc
GRE

Great writers & kids
write mystery stories

	DATE DUE		
10/99			